Tammy's Tearoom

CW00498162

By Michel

Dedication

To Paul Watters for letting me publish one of his many wonderful recipes in my story.

Thank you.

To Mary for your last-minute help.

To the thousands of people who never got to find out about their lost family.

Author's note

Check out the recipe at the end of the book courtesy of renowned chef Paul Watters.

This time it's a recipe for the sweeter tooth.

Copyright

Seagull Bay
residents of book 2

Ben

Tammy

Declan

Fernando

Chris & Nicola

Katherine

Christening Footprints

Pharis

Reverend Townsend

Paula

Pippa

Oliver

Mina

Ginger   Jess

Christine

Richi

Act one - Chapter one

Tammy felt a tickle on the end of her nose. With her arms tucked away underneath the duvet, and feeling far too cosy to scratch it, in true Bewitched style, she wiggled it, just like Samantha the Witch used to do from her beloved childhood sitcom.

Itch gone, she squirmed around, trying to find a more comfortable position on the small two-seater couch—her new bed for the last ten days. But then the tickle started again. Tammy reluctantly pulled out an arm and rubbed at the tip of her button-shaped nose—a nose her social worker had told her looked exactly like her mother's.

Tammy really hoped the reference was true. However, the only way the social worker would know such a thing was from seeing a photograph of her mother, and as far as she was aware, the only photo that existed of her parents was the one Tammy had, which was a worn-out dog-eared one.

In the photo, her mother was holding Tammy in her arms and looking down lovingly at her newborn baby daughter. Her father stood proudly at her mother's side with his arm wrapped protectively around her shoulders and a smile spread across his face that could light the way home for a thousand fishing boats returning to harbour on a foggy morning.

It was the only possession Tammy had of her parents—the only image, to her knowledge, that proved they had existed and were not just a figment of her imagination.

Occasionally over the years, she had dreams she was sure were memories of her brief time with her parents. There were dreams of them feeding squirrels in the park, or dancing around the sitting room to music on the radio. But she couldn't be certain of whether they were real memories or just made up to satisfy her craving to know more about them.

Tammy had lost them twenty-three years ago when they perished in a gas explosion and house fire when she was just four, so any snippet of information about them was like finding a diamond in a snowdrift.

If it hadn't been for the fact she was poorly in hospital with meningitis, she too would have perished alongside them. It had been a miracle Tammy wasn't with them on that fateful day. But the universe had different plans for Tammy.

She was later told by her social worker that her mother had slept alongside her at the hospital every night since she'd been taken in, refusing to leave her side, but at the insistence of the hospital, had finally gone back home with her father to freshen up and get some clean clothes ready for Tammy's discharge.

She'd been fostered after that and spent most of her childhood and teenage years in three long-term placements. It was a happy childhood, but deep down, she always knew it differed from her friends.

The nose tickle returned, Tammy stuck out her bottom lip and blew up at it this time, her arms too warm below the covers to scratch at it. After a restless night, getting hamstring cramps three times, her body refused to wake up yet.

A small childish giggle made her open one of her eyes to be greeted by a mischievous grin, a splatter of freckles, and a shock of red hair.

'Toby. Where's your mummy?'

The hushed and clearly annoyed voice of Evelyn coming from the hall made Toby's smile instantly vanish. *'Toby! Have you had my lipstick again?'*

Tammy heard her friend Evelyn unsuccessfully tiptoeing in high heels on the laminated hallway floor. Toby heard it too and sucked in a shocked breath, running to hide behind the full-length curtains that grazed the floor beneath the window. Tammy opened her other eye and turned to look at the door as it creaked open. Evelyn's face appeared around it.

Evelyn's eyes widened when they rested on Tammy and her hand shot to her mouth, but it couldn't stifle the laugh escaping through her fingers. 'Oh no. I'm so sorry Tammy. That little rascal has been in my make-up bag again.' Evelyn looked around the sitting room before her eagle eyes rested on the twitching curtain.

She stormed into the room, over to the curtains, and yanked them open. Tammy hissed like a vampire about to meet its demise and raised her arm to cover her eyes.

'Sorry mummy, I was just playing.' Toby's small innocent voice could melt an iceberg. He reached his hand forward and offered Evelyn a mushed-up lipstick and an eyeshadow palette that looked as if a crow's talon had been raking at it.

Evelyn's shoulders dropped. 'Oh Toby, you little imp, that's my brand-new lipstick.' A strangled moan came out of Evelyn's throat. 'And look at the state of you. You're going to be late for nursery now and your sister will be late for school.' Evelyn scooped Toby up and turned her head to look at Tammy. 'Sorry, Tammy. I'll try to keep him out of here tomorrow morning.'

Tammy sat up and rubbed the back of her neck. She felt as though she'd done eight rounds with Mike Tyson. 'It's fine Evelyn. I don't mind. It was your sitting room before I took it over. I really appreciate you putting me up like this. I'm just sorry it's an inconvenience for you all.'

Evelyn blanched. 'You are *not* an inconvenience, Tammy. If that...*ex-boyfriend* of yours hadn't been such a—a...' Evelyn walked towards the door as she spoke. 'Well, I'll not say what's on my mind because little ears are listening, but *he's* the one who should have been out on the streets after what he did to you—turning your life upside down like that overnight. Don't you worry about a thing. You can stay here as long as you need to Tammy.'

'Thank you. You and Tim have been so kind, but I won't put you out for much longer. Hopefully, I'll hear back from one of those jobs I've applied for today, and then I'll be able to get a deposit for a new apartment.'

Evelyn's eyes matched the sympathetic smile on her lips, and it made Tammy's chest go tight. 'You are *not* putting us out, Tammy. I just wished I had an extra bedroom to offer you instead of my couch.'

Nancy moaned from the kitchen, complaining, 'Mommy, this toast is burnt.'

Evelyn's eyes rolled. She pulled her mouth into an over-exaggerated smile. 'Besides, you'd be missing all this *wonderful chaos* if you weren't here.' Tammy laughed. Evelyn dropped her head to the side to look around, a squirming Toby fighting to get out of her arms. 'You know the drill, Tammy. Help yourself to whatever you want in the fridge.' Tammy opened her mouth to object, but Evelyn shook her head to stop her. 'And no. I don't want to hear you offering to pay again.' She winked at Tammy. 'And Tammy, I'd consider taking a shower before you take any Zoom interviews today.' Evelyn giggled just like Toby had earlier, before disappearing through the door.

Tammy threw the duvet back and rose gingerly from her couch-bed, stretching out the kinks of her spine as she did. Walking over to the mirror above the fireplace, her mouth dropped open when she saw her reflection.

She looked like a bad version of the famous Blue face painting by Pablo Picasso. Toby had used her face as an artist's easel. Tammy laughed at first, but then she looked around to the small couch that was now her bed, and tears brimmed on her lower lashes.

Tammy didn't want Evelyn to see her crying. She had been more than supportive by offering her somewhere to stay. In fact, all her friends had. Tammy had gone from one friend to another, couch surfing since her split from Richi, but always moving on before she outstayed her welcome at her generous and kind-hearted friends' homes.

This morning, Tammy felt that the time had come again. Although she knew Evelyn would turn red in the face denying the fact, they both knew that having a grown woman sleeping in the family sitting room was inconvenient—for everyone.

Tammy swiped away the brimming tears before Evelyn walked back in, leaving a crimson streak of lipstick mixed in with silver-grey eyeshadow on the back of her hand. Her mind was made up. She'd find somewhere cheap to rent until she found a job—even if it meant draining the last of her measly savings.

Her hands bunched into fists by her sides as she thought about how naïve she'd been in letting Richi talk her into putting *only* his name on the lease of the apartment and on the bank account of the baking business they'd started *together*.

She'd vowed to herself six months ago, as she sat on her pile of belongings outside the apartment she helped pay for, that it would never happen again. She'd been such a naïve fool—but never again. Once bitten, twice shy, that was her new motto.

Evelyn's breathless voice from out in the hall pulled her from her trance. 'Bye Tammy, I'm in a rush so I'll see you later!'

Tammy turned to look at the door and tried to call out a reply past the lump that had formed in her throat. 'Yes, see you—' the front door slammed shut, '—later.'

A beep from her phone alerted her to a calendar event reminder. Taking one last look at her reflection, she sighed and turned around, her eyes scanning the sitting room for her handbag because little Toby had a habit of hiding it. Thankfully, today wasn't one of those times. She spotted the strap sticking out from the side of her couch-bed.

Pulling her mobile from her bag, Tammy's gut tightened at the thought of receiving an alert for anything related to her lost business. When her life was flying high, she'd pre-set months of business-related alerts on her phone calendar, but since Richi had done the dirty on her, anything concerning him and the business made her feel anxious, so she was still yet to go through her calendar and delete them.

All her friends felt the same way regarding Richi and her lost business. They'd dutifully stood by her side and had boycotted the bakery shop after what Richi did to her. She knew there was no way of claiming back what she'd lost, but it didn't stop her from not caring about her lost business—but not him—he was a pig.

Tapping in her passcode, the home screen flickered on, showing her screen saver as a lovely tropical beach scene. Less than six months ago it had been a photo of Richi and her standing side-by-side with cheesy smiles planted on their faces, a cupcake in each of their hands as they held them up high in front of their new store, marking the celebration of their opening day. The memory was now bittersweet.

Tammy swiped the screen away and opened her calendar. 'Wish Great Uncle Ben a happy seventy-ninth birthday,' she said aloud. She barely knew her great-uncle, but he was the only living relative who kept in touch with her. Her only living grandparents hadn't even bothered to lay claim to her after her parent's untimely deaths. They'd never once visited her at her foster homes.

Tammy was non-the-wiser when she was a child, but it troubled her as she got older and was mature enough to understand the dynamics of the family. She'd dissected herself and wondered what was wrong with her that they'd not wanted anything to do with her—never keeping in touch—especially as her Great-Uncle Ben was the only one to have ever sent her birthday cards.

Tammy searched for Ben's number and hit speed dial. The ringtone purred away, sending Tammy into another dream-like trance. It always took Ben ages to get to the phone. Tammy supposed it was because of his age. Tammy thought of her great-uncle Ben as she waited for him to answer.

The first time she'd ever spoken to him was on her thirteenth birthday when her foster mother had called up to her in her room as she was doing her homework to say that her uncle was on the phone. How surprised she'd been to speak to him in person. Up until then, he'd been just a name on a card and a *very* welcome ten-pound note, which he never missed gifting her throughout her childhood, increasing to twenty pounds when she'd turned sixteen. In return, she'd send him a birthday card, which also turned into an annual telephone call to wish him many happy returns after that surprise thirteenth birthday call.

'Hello. Who is this?'

Tammy's lips curled into a smile on hearing her Uncle Ben's rugged voice. He'd answered the phone with the same question for the last fourteen years since they'd began their annual calls.

'Happy birthday, Great-Uncle Ben. It's Tammy.'

'Ah, Tammy...what a lovely surprise. I was just thinking of you as I served Pippa with her morning fish order. She's around the same age as you, maybe a year or two older.'

Tammy couldn't keep the astonishment from her voice. 'You're working today, Uncle Ben? Even on your birthday?'

Ben's soft laugh spread much-needed warmth around Tammy's heart. 'There's no rest for an old seadog like me. Besides, who would serve the local community their fish if I didn't? The fish they buy from supermarkets is rubbish compared to the fresh catches I sell.' Tammy chuckled. 'I've been thinking Tammy. It would be lovely to see you. I know you have your own busy life, but I have a spare bedroom if you ever want to visit...or even holiday here. You can stay as long as you like,' he paused. 'Or if you don't feel comfortable staying with me, Pippa's family owns a hotel here in Seagull Bay. I'm sure I can bargain a deal with her.'

Tammy sucked in a ragged breath, holding back her tears. It was as if her parents were trying to help her from the other side. She swallowed past the new lump which had miraculously appeared in her throat. 'Yes... I'd really like that Uncle Ben. I'd love to come and visit and stay with you.'

She heard him chuckle with relief. 'That is music to my old ears, lass. When shall I expect to see you?'

Tammy hesitated. 'Is tomorrow too soon?' she asked, biting her bottom lip, nervous for his answer.

'Not soon enough, my dear girl.' Tears trickled down her cheeks. 'I'll put clean bedding on in the spare bedroom.'

'I'm really looking forward to meeting you, Uncle Ben. Is there anything you'd especially like to receive for your birthday gift? A bottle of whiskey perhaps?'

'The only gift that will hold any meaning for me is seeing your lovely face, lass. I must go. Someone is calling from the hut to be served. Bye lass, see you tomorrow.'

The lump in her throat had doubled in size and Tammy just about squeezed out her reply. 'Bye Uncle Ben.'

Tammy ended the call feeling brighter than she had in months. She sighed happily. She hadn't baked since her split from Richi, but now she was filled with hope and optimism, and, bubbling with excitement, she realised she wanted to bake again. This would be the first time she'd baked in six months. She was going to bake a birthday cake for Ben and a batch of cupcakes for Evelyn as a thank you.

An impish grin lit up her face. She'd decorate Toby's cake with icing to match the surprise makeover he'd given her whilst sleeping.

Chapter two

I t had been a tearful departure at the train station, saying her thanks and goodbyes to Evelyn. Somehow, Tammy knew her stay in Seagull Bay was going to be longer than the brief visit she first envisioned. She needed to escape the city and be in a place where there was zero chance of running into Richi—zero chance of running into men full stop.

She found a seat with a table and placed the large container down in front of her. What on Earth had possessed her to make such a big birthday cake was beyond her.

As the train sped through towns and then countryside Tammy gazed out of the window and imagined what type of idyllic lives the residents of the houses that flashed past were living. Were there any facing the same uncertain future she was?

Lost in her thoughts, Tammy almost missed the conductor's announcement of the train's arrival at the station she needed and hastily gathered her belongings. With a large suitcase, a cake box, and her handbag, she struggled off the train and onto the platform where she found a quiet space to book a taxi.

Taxi booked; Tammy took a moment to take in the magnitude of her decision. She was out of the city and away from Richi, but she had also cut off her support—her friends.

Ben might well be family by blood, but in all senses of the word, he was a stranger.

Tammy didn't have time to contemplate her situation any further, because her phone pinged to say her taxi had arrived. Fifteen minutes later, she was paying the driver and standing on the seafront, looking down at the beach six feet below. Inhaling deeply, she filled her lungs with fresh sea air and looked out into the horizon across the ocean, before turning her attention to the squawking of the seagulls lining the cliffs on either side of the Bay, relaxed and at one with nature as the early morning sun beat down on her shoulders.

As the sun penetrated her jacket, Tammy glanced down at the cake container at her feet. Thank goodness she'd decided against using fresh cream in her icing. Still, in this heat, even the buttered frosting would spoil soon if she didn't get it stored in a cool place.

Turning around to view the different coloured houses lining the seafront, Tammy's first impression of Seagull Bay was one of wonderment. Compared to the dreary city she'd left behind Seagull Bay held the promise of something magical. It felt almost as if she had come home, which was an impossible notion, as she'd never visited this part of the country before.

A very handsome man with unruly dark curls walked past whistling with a newspaper curled up under his arm and his hands stuffed into his pockets. He looked at Tammy and flashed her a perfect toothy smile. 'Morning.'

Tammy noticed he had a slight American accent. She smiled back, thinking how out of place he looked here with his designer tan and centrefold good looks.

'Erm, excuse me. But could you point me in the direction of Ben's house, please?'

The man paused and then changed direction to walk towards her. 'Old fisherman Ben?'

Tammy nodded, feeling foolish that she'd omitted to mention his surname. The handsome man studied her intently. 'And who are you?'

Tammy stiffened. Who was he to question her? All she wanted was directions. What was it with men—especially handsome men? 'I don't see how that is any of your concern?'

The man took the paper out from under his arm and crossed his arms. 'Well, let me tell you. A stranger coming into my close-knit community asking about a very dear friend is my concern.'

Tammy's mouth dropped open. 'You're friends with my Great-Uncle Ben?'

Now it was time for the handsome man's jaw to drop open. 'You're related to Ben? I didn't know he had any relations.' He uncrossed his arms and extended his hand. I'm Oliver, the landlord of the pub and hotel, The Cheese Wedge and Pickles. I'm so sorry about the inquisition—I didn't mean to be rude... It's just, with all the tourists that come here, we like to look out for each other.'

Tammy nodded. 'I understand... No that's a lie, I don't. I come from the city. Nobody knows who their neighbour is, let alone looks out for them. By the way, I'm Tammy.'

Oliver nodded, 'Hello Tammy.' He gestured to Tammy's suitcase and cake container. 'So, what brings you here? A holiday with your uncle?'

Tammy shook her head. 'A long-term visit, with a view to moving here permanently if I can find work.' She pointed down at the cake container. 'It was Ben's birthday yesterday, and that's the cake I made him. I didn't expect it to be so hot this early though, so I hope it hasn't melted into a pile of goo.'

Oliver's eyebrows rose. 'Ben kept that quiet. He actually lives on the edge of town, right at the top... I have an idea. Why don't I store your cake in the pub's refrigerator and you can coax Ben down to the pub tonight? We'll have a little celebration for him.'

Tammy was overcome. Other than her friends, she'd never known strangers to be so kind. 'Erm, I can try. I don't even know if he drinks alcohol.'

Oliver chuckled, 'Nor me, he hasn't been to the pub in the three months I've owned it, but we serve non-alcoholic drinks, so he can't give you any excuses when you ask him to come tonight.'

Tammy nodded. 'Okay, that sounds like a lovely plan if I can get him to agree.'

Oliver dipped his head towards a large white pub a little further on and reached for Tammy's suitcase. 'Come on then. Let's put your cake on ice and then I'll drive you to Ben's place. If you hadn't already noticed, this seaside town isn't exactly on the flat.'

'Are you sure?'

'Yes, I'm sure. My fiancé Pippa will see to the cake while I drive you.'

'I don't want to put either of you to any trouble.'

'It's no trouble at all. Come on—this way.' Tammy followed Oliver, keeping half a step back. 'In fact, you're doing me a favour. It will get me out of mopping the cellar. There's a sticky spillage that needs seeing to, but if I help you, I'm hoping Pippa will clean it up.' Oliver chuckled to himself as he led the way.

Tammy's brow drew together. *Men*, she thought, *they are all the same—selfish*.

TEN MINUTES LATER, Tammy raised her hand in a farewell gesture to Oliver as he turned his car around and headed back down the hill. She stared at the small cottage-type terrace house with a wooden lean-to on the right-hand side. The green paint on the windowsills was flaking and there were weeds where flowers should have been growing, but apart from the house needing a lot of TLC, it had a rustic charm about it.

Tammy clutched the handle of her suitcase and walked up the short stone path to the front door. She lifted the tinged green brass knocker that must have shone with polished brilliance at one time in its life and knocked.

Her hands were clammy with nerves. The last time she'd been in the presence of someone who shared her same DNA was when she was four years old.

She stood patiently for a few minutes and was just about to knock again when the wooden door to the lean-to hut opened and a man with a grey bushy beard, blue beanie hat, and blue denim dungarees appeared.

The crinkles of skin surrounding his eyes instantly swallowed them up when his mouth curled up into a smile. 'Tammy...I thought your mother's ghost had come back to visit me for a second there. You are the image of her, but you have your father's colouring. The same coloured hair. What colour are your eyes?'

Tammy was dumbstruck. The last thing she expected was to be told she resembled her parents. 'Bl-blue.'

'Yep. You got your father's eyes alright. Nicola's eyes were green.'

Tammy's heart galloped in her chest. She always thought her father's eyes were grey. The photo was old and dirty. Over the years, her sticky little fingers had clutched it too tightly as she spent hour after hour examining every detail. If she never got to hear another word about her parents, those extra titbits of information would nourish her soul for years to come. But Ben was standing before her. He was the fountain of knowledge, and she was thirsty for more.

Yet, her unquenchable thirst would have to wait. She couldn't be rude. She dragged her suitcase back down the path and made her way over to Ben, releasing the suitcase's handle to open her arms wide when she was a couple of feet from him and embrace her elderly uncle.

'It's so lovely to meet you Great-Uncle Ben.' It surprised Tammy at how sturdy he felt beneath her embrace. She was expecting someone of seventy-nine to be skin and bone. He smelt like fresh fish, but Tammy couldn't imagine him smelling any other way. Strangely, it was welcoming.

Ben held her at arm's length. 'You don't know how good it is to see you, Tammy. The last time I laid eyes on you, you were just a few days old.'

'Really? You've met me before?' Tammy was taken aback. 'Did you visit my parents in the city?'

Ben chuckled and shook his head. 'I've never been further than York Cathedral. No. I was much too busy with work to venture outside of town. Your parents used to live here in Seagull Bay.' It was a good job Ben was still holding onto Tammy because she felt a little dizzy. 'Anyway, we can chat more in a little while. Let's get you settled and I'll stick the kettle on for a brew.'

Ben turned around and led the way through the lean-to hut. It smelt just as fishy as he did. It was sparse inside the hut. There was a large chest freezer, a smaller one, a wooden stool, and a wooden cart that looked like a large wheelbarrow, but with four wheels instead of three.

At the end of the hut was a door that led to a small kitchen inside the house. The kitchen was simple and tiny, but Tammy felt as though she'd gone back in time. She tried to put an age to the basic cupboard units, but she'd never visited any museums that paid homage to the past eras of Great Britain, so she could only guess, and her mind settled for the fifties.

Ben continued through another door, which led into a narrow and dimly lit hallway. He raised his arm and pointed up the stairs. 'Your room is the door immediately to your right at the top of the stairs. The bathroom is the door next to it if you want to freshen up. I'll put the kettle on, lass.'

'Thank you, Uncle Ben. Yes, I'll quickly freshen up.' Ben nodded and disappeared back into the kitchen. Tammy pushed the extendable handle down on her suitcase and carried it slowly up the stairs.

Her mouth tugged up at the corners when she saw that the well-worn rectangles of carpet on the stairs didn't cover the entire steps. There were five or six inches of the stained wood staircase on either side of the steps that had a small gathering of dust up the corners. The seventh step creaked, and it only added to the charm of the worn-out staircase.

Twisting the wooden doorknob on the first door on the right, Tammy pushed it open and was immediately immersed in sunlight. The room wasn't anything like she was expecting. She'd expected it to be as dimly lit as the hallway with something like a bottle green or rustic brown woollen blanket on the bed, but the room was far from dull. It was painted in a cheerful pale lemon with an even brighter flower-patterned bedspread. It even had a small potted plant on the windowsill.

Tammy pulled her suitcase over the threshold and wheeled it over to the wooden set of drawers. She thought she really should unpack but then changed her mind. She'd do it later. Her clothes couldn't get more crumpled than they already were. Besides, she was eager to get back to Uncle Ben and listen to anything he could tell her about her parents. She'd use the bathroom and unpack later.

Tammy's smile was even bigger when she saw the colour of the bathroom suite. Mint green suited the tiny room. It even smelt of mint—mint and lemon disinfectant.

By the time Tammy was washing her hands, the high-pitched sound of a whistling kettle and the promise of a cup of tea was calling to her.

She made her way downstairs, and when she reached the creaky step, Ben called out from the kitchen. 'Go into the sitting room, Tammy. We'll have our tea in there.'

Tammy smiled to herself. Her uncle must know every groan of his cosy cottage. She twisted her head, saw an open door, and headed for it.

The sitting room was totally in keeping with the rest of the house. It had two armchairs, a small coffee table and a sideboard with two radios. One looked old, but how old, she didn't have a clue. But the other was modern. Not from this decade, but a good deal younger than its companion.

There was a stack of newspapers at the side of the armchair with threadbare arms. Tammy knew without a doubt that was Ben's armchair. Like her uncle, the sitting room also had the remnants of a fish smell, but it wasn't unpleasant—it was her uncle's smell.

Tammy heard the rattle of the tray behind her and stepped out of the way. 'Go on, sit down. Don't be shy. You've been in this sitting room before you know. That was almost three decades ago mind you, but you've been here before, nonetheless.'

Tammy's chest fluttered with the statement as she settled into the other armchair and Ben placed the tray down. There were two unmatching mugs on it, a china teapot with a chipped lid, a small sterling silver pot with milk in it, a couple of sachets of sugar that looked like they'd come from a café, and a blue plate with garibaldi biscuits on it. Tammy grinned and watched enthralled as her Uncle Ben sunk into his armchair with a contented sigh, his eyes twinkling as he looked across at her.

'This is one of the happiest days of my life,' he said, breaking into a smile. Tammy was overcome with emotion and had to blink away tears that took her completely by surprise.

'Can you tell me more about my parents, Uncle Ben?'

'I certainly can. But before I do, tell me how *you* are? I don't know the grown-up Tammy, but I sense sadness in you my gal.'

Those few kind words from a blood relation were all it took. The dam that had been strong and steady up until now, finally burst.

Chapter three

B en hadn't interrupted once as Tammy had poured her heart out about how Richi had cheated on her and then told her she had to leave their apartment, and that she couldn't do a thing about it because his name was the only one on the lease. But worse, how he'd also tricked her with their business by putting everything in his name as well. He'd made it impossible for her to lay claim to any of it—even the profits they'd both helped the business make—the bank account was solely in his name.

When she was done, Ben got up from his chair and walked over to her, offering his upturned hands. Tammy looked at them as she swiped away her tears with the backs of her hands before placing her hands in his. Ben pulled her out of the chair and into his arms. Tammy was almost a head taller than him and had to bend her neck to place her cheek on his shoulder, but it was the best hug she'd ever had in her life. He patted her back tenderly without saying a word.

Tammy was amazed by how natural the embrace felt. She'd been in her uncle's company for less than an hour and here she was, spilling her heart out and soaking his shoulder in salty tears.

'If only I was thirty years younger, I'd catch the train to wherever that young man is and I'd give him a piece of my mind...and maybe a knuckle sandwich, too.'

Ben's sincere words made Tammy's chest tighten, but his knuckle sandwich comment drew out a chuckle she couldn't stop from dancing up her throat.

She started giggling and lifted her head from her Uncle Ben's shoulder to look down into his kind blue eyes. 'Thank you for making me feel so much better Uncle Ben. That's the first time in months I've genuinely laughed.'

Ben smiled widely. 'See. You were meant to come visit me. Now, how about that tea? A nice cup of tea makes everything a little better.' He turned around to pour the tea. 'Blimey. It's stone cold.' Tammy laughed harder. 'How about we gander down to Katherine's café for a cuppa instead? I can show you the sights on the way, and we can talk some more about your parents?'

Tammy nodded enthusiastically, feeling as if she were a young child again, and filled with enthusiasm for a new world.

TEN MINUTES LATER, Tammy and Ben were making their way down the steep narrow road from Ben's house into town. Tammy drew her brow together as she wondered how on Earth her Uncle Ben made this journey daily. It was bad enough going downhill—she was dreading the walk back. Baking cakes wasn't exactly the most energetic job to have, and she hadn't even done that in the last six months. Her Uncle Ben must be as fit as a horse.

She turned to look at her uncle as they walked. 'Do you use the wooden cart I saw in your lean-to hut to get and sell your fish uncle?'

'I do indeed. I fill it with ice and take it down to the dock where I buy the best of the early morning catch from the local fishermen. Then I stay by the dock and sell most of it there. Whatever's left I bring back to the hut and freeze it to sell from there.' Tammy's jaw dropped open as she tried to picture her little uncle manhandling the cart filled with ice. 'I used to be one of those fishermen you know Tammy.' He stopped walking and looked at her with a solemn stare. 'That's why I couldn't take you on when you were orphaned. Well, that and the fact I was a single man in my fifties. I'm sorry if you ever felt I let you down.'

Tammy's eyebrows shot up. 'Goodness no, Uncle Ben, that's never once crossed my mind. In all honesty, it was up to my grandparents to take me on, but for some reason they abandoned me. But I had a good childhood, anyway. I had three long-term foster placements with lovely carers.' Tammy hesitated before asking, 'Do you know anything about them? My grandparents?'

Ben huffed and continued to walk on. Tammy caught him up in two paces. 'I'm sorry to say this aloud, Tammy, but your mother's parents were scum. They were selfish drug users. They dumped your poor mother onto anyone who'd have her so they could go off partying. Your mum lived with me for a short while when she was young. I would have loved to have her permanently, but with my job, I was up at the crack of dawn and out to sea.'

Tammy was overwhelmed with the news. 'So, mom lived with you? Was it in the same house you're living in now?'

'Yes. She stayed in the room you have.' Warmth spread throughout Tammy from her fingers to her toes. 'Your father was grandparent reared. I honestly don't know what happened to his parents. I don't think he did either.'

Tammy gasped. 'Wow.'

They got to the bottom of the hill and Ben pointed over to a large white building. 'And that is where your parents used to date—The Cheese Wedge and Pickles.'

'Oh my goodness. They met here in Seagull Bay?'

'Yes, your parents lived in the next village over at the time, but your mum would come here as much as she could. She was born here and Seagull Bay was home to her.'

'That's Oliver and Pippa's pub, isn't it?'

Ben's brow rose. 'Yes, how do you know that?'

'I met Oliver earlier. I asked him if he knew you so I could get directions, and he offered me a lift. He wants us to go to the pub this evening.' She gave her uncle her sweetest smile. 'Can we go Uncle Ben? I'd love to see where mum and dad met.'

'To be honest, I don't go there much. Maybe the odd times around Christmas. You see, I have to get up early to get the fish. The locals rely on me to buy it, otherwise, they'd have to get it from those awful supermarkets—big corporate-owned places that only think about making profit for their shareholders... No, I have to be there for the locals.' Tammy could see her uncle talking himself out of it. She needed to persuade him. His birthday cake was there. 'Please, uncle. We can just have one drink and stay for an hour at the most.'

Ben turned to look at Tammy with a wry smile. 'You can wrap me around your little finger just like your mother used to.' Tammy's tummy fluttered. Ben nodded with a chuckle. 'Alright. I'll come for one drink. But right now, the drink I need more than anything is a cup of hot tea.'

Tammy leaned over and kissed him on the cheek. 'Thank you.'

The little café they were heading for looked so different from the bakery store she'd opened with Richi. The charming little café was nestled in between two other shops which led down to the seafront. It had whitewashed walls and blue gingham curtains halfway up the windows, framed by window boxes bursting with colourful flowers, perfectly complementing the coastal surroundings and different coloured houses that dotted the steep streets beyond it. Outside, the frontage had half a dozen small round tables shaded by striped umbrellas, all but one filled with people chatting away and idling in the mid-day sun.

As they got closer, Tammy could see a weathered blue door, which was propped open by a patchwork dog doorstop. The scents of home-cooked food and freshly brewed coffee inviting passersby. Above it hung a driftwood sign with the café's name, Katherine's Café, painted in swooping blue italics.

Sitting on the tables outside the café, customers had the perfect vantage point, allowing them to sip their beverages while enjoying ocean views and the sound of the waves rolling against the shore and the chatter of seagulls.

With its breezy, welcoming vibe and idyllic seaside setting, the café emanated a cheerful yet peaceful charm. It was Tammy's kind of heaven.

She noticed a wooden bone-shaped sign in the window before they entered.

DOGS ARE WELCOME.

It was a nice touch and obviously great for business, as almost every other customer had a dog at their feet, or if small enough, on their laps.

There were fewer people inside, but it was still busy. Ben pointed to an empty table by the window. 'Go and sit yourself down. I'll get the tea.'

Tammy nodded with a smile and sat down looking about her and daydreaming about her parents having one of their first dates in the café.

Inside was equally as charming. The same chequered blue and white was on the plastic tablecloths that adorned each table. Tammy's eyes wandered and she imagined what she'd do to the place if it was hers. Maybe a lick of paint, flowers on the tables, and pictures on the walls. The only thing that was hanging on the wall at the moment was a cork notice board. She squinted her eyes to read the cards pinned on it.

Mamas & Papas pushchair for sale.
Almost new. £300 o.n.o.
Call or text Yvonne. 07893 672973

...

Dog walking.
Any size. Any Breed.
Call Tom to discuss rates. 07563 479224

Tammy's eyes lifted to a colourful poster.

Business for rent.

Katherine's Café.
Established café business currently open 6 days a week from 6 AM to 3 PM.
Short-term rental of 18 months with a view to renting long term.
Contact Katherine on 07986 7456244
Or see Katherine at the counter.

Tammy's heart began beating quickly. It was as if fate had led her here. Was it still available? If it was, could she afford it? She was literally down to her last few hundred pounds. She chewed on her bottom lip, deep in thought.

'Penny for them?'

Ben placed two mugs down on the table.

Tammy pointed over to the sign. 'It's for rent Uncle Ben. Or at least I hope it still is.'

Ben slowly turned his head in the direction Tammy was pointing. 'What am I looking at? I need my reading glasses.'

'It says this café is up for rent Uncle Ben. Do you know anything about it?'

Ben looked thoughtful. 'I don't know that I do.' He swivelled in his chair to look towards the counter. 'Katherine!'

An elderly lady with a kind smile appeared from out the back and swept her head over the faces in the café, looking for the person who'd called her name. She stopped when Ben's hand rose, motioning her over. 'Ah, it's you, Ben.' She came from behind the counter and walked over to their table, smiling at Tammy when she reached it. 'So, is this lovely young lady your great-niece, Ben?'

Tammy smiled as Ben nodded, his face beaming. 'Yes, this is Tammy.'

Tammy did a little wave. 'Hello. Katherine, it's nice to meet you.'

'It's. lovely to meet you too, Tammy. You know. The only way I ever know it's Ben's birthday is when he tells me you've called.'

Tammy felt a wave of guilt. She only ever called him on his birthday. Why hadn't she called him more often? He was probably lonely. Maybe she deserved what she got from Richi for being so selfish and wrapped up in her own little bubble.

She joined in with the playful ribbing directed at her uncle. 'So he told you about my call yesterday, then?'

Katherine's hands flew up to her cheeks. 'No, he didn't.' She looked accusingly at Ben. 'Why didn't you tell me it was your birthday, Ben? I would have cooked you a full English breakfast—on the house no less.'

Ben brushed away her comment with a flick of his hand and a puff of his lips. 'I wouldn't let a young woman like yourself do that.'

Katherine roared with laughter. 'Young woman? I bet there's barely five years between us, Ben.'

Ben chuckled and crossed his arms. 'Well, I'm not disclosing my age and I know a lady never tells hers, so let's leave it at that.'

Katherine nodded. 'Fair enough, but your next breakfast is on me and I'm not taking no for an answer.'

Tammy saw an opportune moment to ask about the sign. She pointed towards the corkboard. 'Is the café still for rent, Katherine?'

Katherine pursed her lips together and wobbled her head. 'Hmmm. I'm not sure my love. I had an enquiry a few weeks ago and the person I spoke to appeared to be very interested, but I haven't heard anything back yet. I'm a little worried too, because I have to wrap things up here soon and move back to my hometown to care for my elderly mother. I really don't want to close the place because I still need some income, and renting it was the best option.' She smiled at Tammy. 'Why love? Do you know anyone who is interested?'

Tammy matched Katherine's smile. 'Yes. Me.'

A man at the counter called out. '*Service*!'

Katherine looked back over her shoulder and tutted. 'Tourists have no patience.' She turned her attention back to Tammy. 'I'll tell you what, I'll find out his number and call him back. I need to know for certain anyway, and then we can get together for a chat if it's still free, eh?'

Tammy nodded enthusiastically. 'Wonderful. Also, would you like to join us this evening at The Cheese Wedge and Pickles, Katherine? We're going for a drink.'

Katherine's face lit up. 'I would. What time will you be there?'

Tammy looked across at Ben for an answer.

'7 o'clock,' he said. 'I need to be in bed for nine.'

Katherine nodded. 'Lovely. I'll look forward to it.' Her smile broadened as she turned around and walked back over to the counter.

Tammy watched her go and then looked back at Ben. He looked like a cat who'd just drank a pot of cream. 'You look happy Uncle Ben. Is it because I invited Katherine to come along this evening?'

He shook his head, his smile not wavering. 'I'm ecstatic you are thinking of staying on here longer than the short visit I thought you were only coming for.'

Tammy grimaced. 'It all depends on whether I can get a job and find somewhere to live though, uncle.'

'Poppycock! You can stay with me as long as you want. And don't worry about food. I have a freezer full of fish.'

Tammy burst out laughing. 'Will it be kippers for breakfast, cod for lunch, and lobster for supper?' she ended with a wink.

'Something like that. Anyway, I'm just happy I'll get to see more of you.'

'Me too.' Tammy reached across the table and squeezed Ben's hand just as a young man walked past, looking down at the gesture with animated shock.

He met Tammy's eyes. 'Have I come on the wrong day? Is this sugar day? Get it?' He pointed at Ben and opened his hands wide, gesturing to the café as he winked at Tammy.

Tammy screwed her face up. She was totally anti-men at the moment and this man's childish insinuation boiled her blood. 'Grow up!'

His face blanched, and he raised his palms at her in defensive as he shook his hands. 'No, no, no. I was only joking.'

He turned to look at Ben with appealing eyes. 'You know what my humour's like don't you Mr Hickman?'

Ben nodded his head with a wry smile. 'Yes, but I told you it would get you in trouble one of these days Pharis, didn't I? I think you owe my great niece an apology.'

Pharis looked at Tammy with a bashful grimace. 'I'm truly sorry if I offended you...'

'Tammy' Ben offered.

'Tammy,' repeated Pharis.

Tammy straightened in her seat. 'It's fine, but maybe next time, think before you speak.'

Pharis nodded his head like a bobby dog toy on the dashboard of a car. 'Yes-yes. I will.' He smiled through thin lips and quickly made his way to the counter.

Tammy shook her head as she looked at her uncle. 'Men.'

'You mean, *young* men,' he smiled.

She looked at the man she'd spoken to maybe just fifteen times in as many years and her heart swelled with love. 'Yes, Uncle Ben...young men.'

Chapter four

Tammy was nervous about entering The Cheese Wedge and Pickles. She didn't know why. But, once inside, her gut warning made sense, because as soon as Ben stepped into the lounge of the pub, the entire room called out in chorus. 'Happy birthday Ben!'

Tammy smiled self-consciously by his side as men approached Ben to shake his hand and women kissed him on the cheek. Oliver came from behind the bar and walked over to them with a dazzling smile.

'It's nice to see you in here, Ben. I don't think you've been into the pub yet since Pippa and I bought it.' He turned to look at Tammy. 'Well done for persuading him. I didn't think you would.'

Tammy smiled back. 'He was trying to get out of it, but he said he'd come for an hour.'

A pretty woman with long brown hair joined Oliver at his side. Oliver slid his arm around her waist and kissed the top of her head. 'Tammy, this is my fiancé, Pippa. Pippa, this is the owner of that enormous mouth-watering cake in the kitchen's refrigerator. This is Ben's great-niece.'

Pippa's face lit up. 'Tammy. Wow! Ben mentions you often when I go to buy my fish from him.'

Tammy's heart swelled at the knowledge she was so special to her uncle that he would talk about her to other people.

Tammy chatted with Pippa, immediately taking a liking to her warm, bubbly personality. Someone touched Tammy's elbow and Pippa smiled at them. 'Good evening, Katherine. Have you found anyone to rent your café yet?'

Tammy turned around to greet Katherine. 'Ah, Katherine. I'm so glad you came.'

'Good evening, ladies.' Katherine smiled at them both and then turned to look at Ben who was sipping a pint of stout and talking to someone on his left, but he hadn't noticed her arrival. She turned her attention back to Pippa and glanced at Tammy as she answered. 'I've had two enquiries so far, Pippa.'

Pippa sighed happily. 'Ah, that's good.' She placed a hand on the top of Katherine's arm and squeezed. 'You'll soon be back with your mum. Excuse me, ladies, I can see Oliver waving his arms at me like an octopus. I think he needs some help behind the bar. It's busier in here than normal.' Pippa strode off towards the bar.

Tammy offered Katherine a seat and they sat down together. Ben's face lit up when he saw Katherine. 'Good evening, Katherine my dear. Can I get you a drink?'

'Evening Ben. I'd love a sloe gin with lemonade, please.'

Ben looked at Tammy. 'Tammy? Do you want another one?'

'Another white wine please, Uncle Ben.'

'Coming right up.'

Tammy watched her uncle make his way to the bar, the standing customers moving to the side to let him pass. She smiled to herself. She could see how much he was well-liked and respected.

'I have great news!' Katherine announced, her eyes twinkling. 'The other interested party backed out of leasing my café. So, if you're still interested, it's yours.'

Tammy could hardly contain her excitement. 'I'm definitely still interested, Katherine.'

'Is that what you do, Tammy? Are you a chef?'

Tammy grimaced and lifted her shoulders. 'Not a chef...I'm a baker. I own—' She stopped to correct herself. '—Until recently, I owned a bakery. I know it's not quite the same thing, but my heart is in catering—whatever food I might serve.'

'Well, if you decide to rent my café, you can serve whatever food you like. It will be your business.'

Tammy's tummy came alive with invisible butterflies. She hadn't felt the flutter of excitement and hope for a long time. 'I really am interested Katherine, but what is the rental amount?'

'With the bills added in with the rent, it will be three hundred pounds per week,' Katherine replied.

Tammy's face fell slightly, and so did the invisible butterflies in her tummy. With the savings she had, she could only cover half that amount for the first month.

Ben appeared at the table at the tail end of the conversation as he placed the drinks down in front of the ladies. Seeing Tammy's disappointment, he placed a hand on her shoulder. 'Don't you worry about a small thing like money. I'll gladly cover the whole rent for the month. Keep what you have for stock. You'll be doing both Katherine and the community a favour by taking on the café.'

Tammy looked up into her uncle's kind blue eyes and shook her head. 'I can't possibly take your money Uncle Ben. No, I-I'll sort it out one way or another.'

Her uncle's grip on her shoulder tightened slightly. 'No. I insist. Please don't say no. You did ask me what I wanted for my birthday, and this is my birthday wish—to help you out.'

Tammy's mouth curled into a smile. 'You've got me there uncle.' She jumped to her feet and wrapped her arms around him, enveloping him in a warm embrace. 'If you're sure, Uncle Ben. I promise I'll pay you back as soon as I can.'

Ben chuckled. 'Of course I'm sure.'

Tammy blinked away the tears. 'Thank you.'

Just then, Pharis sauntered over, holding a tray of drinks. 'Thought I'd buy you all a round of drinks,' he said with a roguish wink. Tammy hadn't even seen him come into the pub.

Though she's noticed on their first encounter how ruggedly handsome he was, after her last relationship disaster, she was wary of *all* men within her own age range. She scolded herself for even noticing how Pharis' smile was cute and lopsided.

Ben shook his head at the offer of another drink. 'Sorry Pharis. It's a lovely gesture, but I have to decline.' He dipped his head towards the table and his half-drunk pint of stout. 'One drink is enough for me.'

Pharis nodded. 'Fair enough Ben. I'm normally a Guinness drinker, but I'm sure I can manage a pint of stout.' He lifted the glass of wine from his tray and offered it to Tammy. 'A truce and a dry white wine for the lady. Oliver told me what you ordered earlier.'

Tammy eyed the drink warily. If she accepted it, would he think she liked him? 'Thank you.' She hoped by accepting the drink the man wouldn't think she liked him in an attraction sort of way.

'Katherine. I know your choice of poison is sloe gin.'

Katherine laughed and happily accepted another gin and lemonade. 'Thank you Pharis. How're your mum and dad? I usually pop into the farm shop every other week, but I haven't been for the last month.'

'Oh, we are really busy at the farm at the moment. Mum's trying to organise a community barbecue again. She said it won't be the same without Marie, Pippa's mother, but that she's had a few requests from the locals for it to start up again this year.'

Tammy had never known such a close-knit community. Across the lounge, Pippa caught Tammy's eye and waved her over discreetly. 'Erm, can you excuse me?'

Tammy glanced back at her Uncle Ben, but he was too busy chatting to someone on his left. Pippa pointed over to a door marked 'kitchen' and they met in front of it.

'The cake you made is on the table in there. The chef has found some candles for you.'

'Aww, that's very kind of him.'

'Yes, Declan is a lovely guy. Go on through, Tammy.'

'Thanks Pippa.'

When Tammy entered the kitchen, she stopped short at the sight of the chef. Tall dark and handsome was an understatement. Muscular, with warm blue eyes and a killer smile, Tammy's knees actually went weak. She thought that only happened in movies. Taken aback by Declan's handsome looks, she was surprised to feel another flutter of attraction so soon after her breakup. What was it with her? First

Oliver—but thankfully he was engaged to Pippa—then Pharis, and now Declan. Men were a no-go. She had specifically banned them from her future.

'You must be Tammy,' Declan said amiably. 'I'm Declan, the chef here. That cake of yours looks incredible!' He handed her some candles and Tammy's stomach did a loop the loop when their hands touched. 'Where did you buy it from?'

Tammy found it difficult to tear her eyes from his, but she did so under duress and began to add the candles to the frosting. 'I made it... I'm a baker.'

'Wow! I take my chef's hat off to you.'

He handed her a kitchen lighter. 'Thanks.' Tammy wanted to talk more about her baking, but that would mean discussing her ex and how he'd taken control of the business they'd started together and for some reason, she didn't want to appear foolish to Declan. She scolded herself in her head for the way she was acting.

He's a man Tammy. Avoid him with a barge pole...and while you're at it, don't accept any more drinks from the ruggedly handsome Pharis either.

'How old is Ben?'

'Seventy-nine. But keep that information close to your chest. I don't think he wants the fact that he's almost eighty years old common knowledge.'

Declan whistled. 'Jeez, he's good for his age. No worries, the secret's safe with me.' Tammy chanced a glance at Declan and regretted it immediately as the blue pools of his eyes sucked hr in again. 'I guess there's something to be said about a fish diet, eh?'

Tammy smiled. 'He has a freezer full. I'm expecting to be served fish for breakfast, lunch, and supper while I stay with him.'

'Oh, so you're staying with Ben while you visit?'

'Yes, my short visit is actually becoming a long-term one now.'

Declan's brow lifted, quizzing. 'Really. How come?'

'I'm taking on the rental lease at Katherine's café.'

Declan's enormous smile made Tammy's breath catch in her throat. 'Nice. I'll definitely be dining more there now.'

Tammy didn't know how to feel about Declan's blatant admittance to finding her attractive in not so many words. 'I-I'd better get these candles lit. Uncle Ben will be wondering where I've got to.'

Tammy lit the candles and Declan walked over to the door to open it for her. Even though Tammy remembered noticing upon entering the kitchen that it was on a swing both ways hinge like she'd had in her bakery, she was still impressed by his gentlemanliness. Once she'd passed through the door, to Tammy's surprise, Declan quickly side-stepped her and called for silence.

'Quiet everyone!'

With the music turned off, silence fell over the customers in the lounge. All eyes turned in Tammy's direction and she felt mini volcanos erupt underneath her cheeks. She was livid inside at Declan for causing such a fuss. He should have asked her first. Tammy had wanted to slip past everyone and wish her uncle a happy birthday privately.

Tammy tentatively walked over to the table where her Uncle Ben and Katherine were sitting. She presented the cake to a very touched Ben.

'Erm, happy birthday Uncle Ben.'

She placed the candlelit cake down in front of her Great-Uncle Ben and he sat motionless, a look of pure astonishment on his weathered face. His mouth hung slightly open, and his eyes glistened under the warm glow of the flames.

'I...I don't know what to say,' Ben stammered, placing his hand on his chest. He glanced around at the smiling faces gathered around him, then back to Tammy. 'You did this for me?'

Tammy nodded, her own eyes welling up with tears. 'Of course, Uncle Ben. I wanted you to feel special today.'

Ben shook his head in wonder, tears now trickling down his cheeks into his bushy beard. He blew out the candles and everyone cheered. Standing up, he stepped out from the table to pull Tammy into a tight embrace.

'You've made this old man very happy,' he said, his voice thick with emotion. As they parted, he wiped at his eyes and chuckled. 'Goodness me, you've got me blubbering like a baby in front of everyone.' He wiped his tears away. 'Thank you, Tammy. What a lovely surprise. I hope it's kipper flavour.' Tammy giggled.

The crowd erupted in warm laughter. Beaming bright enough to light up the whole pub, Ben enthusiastically began shaking hands, hugging, and thanking the many well-wishers flocked around him.

Katherine leaned over to Tammy's ear. 'For a man normally so reserved, seeing Ben radiate pure joy is a beautiful sight to behold. Well done, Tammy. This is a birthday he will never forget.' A lump formed in Tammy's throat. She felt as though she finally felt what it was like to have family—real family. 'Three cheers for Ben!' shouted Katherine. 'Hip-hip.'

The whole pub chorused hooray, and Tammy joined in.

'Hip-hip.'

'Hooray!'

'Hip-hip.'

'Hooray!'

Applause erupted again and a golden retriever and black labrador came bounding over to the table, their noses in the air sniffing and their tails wagging frantically, followed by a frantic-looking Pippa.

'No. You can't eat sugar. It's not good for you.' She grabbed their collars and hauled them away. 'Come on, let's take you upstairs and you can have a slice of beef each.'

Tammy watched her uncle as he made his way around the lounge, her mouth upturned. It was only then that she noticed two sets of eyes watching her from opposite sides of the pub. One set was hazel brown, the other sky blue.

Chapter five

Tammy awoke slowly, blinking against rays of morning sunlight streaming in through lace curtains. Disorientated, for a moment, she was unsure of where she was. She didn't feel the usual aches and pains she'd experienced each morning for the last six months whilst couch hopping amongst her friends. Instead, she could hear the squawk of seagulls in the distance. The previous day suddenly came rushing back to her.

She was in her Great-Uncle Ben's cottage in the charming seaside town of Seagull Bay. More specifically, Tammy was nestled in the very bedroom her mother had slept in as a child. Her smile reached from ear to ear.

Running her hands over the quilted bedspread, Tammy felt a surreal sense of closeness to the mother she'd lost at the tender age of four years old. This room was the nearest thing to a connection she'd ever had. In fact, apart from her treasured tattered and dog-eared photo, this cottage was the nearest connection she'd had to both of her parents. They'd both been here—with her—as a family.

Overcome by bittersweet emotion, Tammy made a silent promise to make her parents proud of her whilst she was in Seagull Bay.

After washing up and getting dressed for the day, she headed downstairs to the cosy little kitchen to make a cup of tea. She called out for her Uncle Ben until she remembered he was a *very* early riser. He'd probably been awake hours before her. She headed into the small kitchen and spotted a note on the kitchen table beside a shiny new key.

Tammy,

I'm down at the harbour selling my wares.

Here is the spare key. Have a great day!

Uncle Ben

Tammy smiled. She felt so at home here already. She'd add the note to the treasured birthday cards he'd sent her throughout her life. They were in a shoebox with the photo of her parents, a small stuffed bear, and the dress she'd been wearing when she was taken into care after her parent's death. Ben was down by the harbour already selling the morning's catch. She would go and say hello and take a photo of him with his cart to keep as her new screen saver.

Pocketing the key to the cottage, instead of making tea herself, Tammy decided to head to the café for tea and a hearty breakfast to go with it. She also wanted a chat with Katherine about preparations for the takeover. She stepped outside into the crisp, salty air.

The cottage sat atop a grassy cliff overlooking the town and the sea below, giving it a perfect vantage point. Tammy paused for a moment, breathing in the invigorating ocean air. The British sea wasn't quite azure, but it glittered all the same under the morning sun, and the blue sky was a riot of seagulls swooping in front of the cliffs on either side of the bay. Tammy had never seen so many in all of her life. She smiled widely.

No wonder it was called Seagull Bay. She gasped in awe at the scene. It was a beautiful day. She hadn't thought about a day like this in such a long time.

As she strolled down the street towards the bay, a motorbike peeled around the corner, pulling up alongside her. Tammy stepped back startled until she recognised the brilliant blue eyes of the rider—even before he removed his helmet. It was Declan, the handsome chef she'd met last night.

He switched off his engine and unclipped the strap under his chin, pulling off the helmet in one swift motion. 'Fancy running into you here!' Declan said with a toothy white grin. His hair was cut buzz short, and now Tammy knew why as she admired the design on his helmet. 'Did Ben enjoy his cake?'

Tammy bristled. What was he insinuating? That she wasn't a very good baker?

She knew he was only being friendly, but Tammy was trying to find an excuse—any excuse—not to like him.

'He said it was the best cake he'd ever tasted,' she said defensively.

Declan ran his tongue around his lips and Tammy's eyes couldn't help but follow the tip of it. 'I agree. I cut myself a slice to try when you nipped to the lady's room just before you left.'

Tammy's mouth dropped open, and she did her best to hide the grin desperate to form on her lips. 'Hey, cheeky!'

Declan's laugh was a smoky velvet that stroked at her skin. She wrapped her arms around her body to protect herself from his charm. She was off men—she mustn't forget—she needed to protect her injured heart.

'Where are you off to so early?'

Tammy was reluctant to tell Declan her plans. It would mean going into detail about why she was here and why she was taking on Katherine's café. In the end, she decided she would tell Declan about the café. She'd tell him she *might* be taking over just in case he was a regular customer. She didn't want to make things awkward explaining why she'd taken over if she had to serve him in front of other local residents.

'I'm going to have breakfast in Katherine's café because I need to familiarise myself with the cuisine, just in case I get to take on the lease.'

'What? You might be taking over Katherine's café? But didn't you say you were a baker, not a chef? You don't have any experience, do you?'

The vein that always appeared when Tammy was holding back her emotions pinged out on her forehead. This time she knew Declan was definitely insinuating she couldn't do the job. 'It's not exactly rocket science is it, frying up a few rashers of bacon and scrambling eggs?!'

Possibly sensing the change in dynamics, Declan glanced at his watch. 'Well, I'd best get to the pub and start prepping for the lunch crowd,' he said, slipping his helmet back on and clipping the strap. 'Maybe I'll see you around later.' With a friendly wave, he sped off down the street.

Letting out a breath she didn't know she'd been holding. Tammy reminded herself that while Declan was distractingly handsome, she knew nothing about him. With her track record, she couldn't trust her judgement. It was best to keep Declan at arm's length, no matter how alluring his smile might be.

As Tammy reached the bottom of the hill, she was amazed by the buzz of activity on the beachfront at such an early hour. Her Uncle Ben wasn't hard to miss. He was surrounded by three women, pointing at fish on his cart and laughing at something witty he must have said. She watched him for a moment as he interacted with them. Anyone could see he loved his job. No wonder he'd never totally retired from the fish trade. Tammy guessed he must really miss the fishing side of it.

Taking her phone out from her pocket, she aimed it at him happily surrounded by his customers. His grey beard bobbed about as he joked with the women, and Tammy caught him in a wonderful pose with a fish in each hand as he held them up, offering them to one of the women to inspect. Turning around with an enormous grin on her face, she headed for the café.

The bells above the door announced her arrival with a merry jingle. Katherine looked up from wiping down the gleaming countertop and smiled. 'Good morning, Tammy.'

'Morning Katherine.'

'I wondered if you'd be in today.' Katherine ushered Tammy over to a table by the front window. 'Sit right there. You have the perfect vantage point to people-watch. Drink?'

'Oo yes, I'd love a strong tea with milk, but no sugar.'

Katherine nodded. 'Have you eaten yet?' Tammy shook her head. 'Okay. Say no more. I'll make you my special.' Before Tammy could object, Katherine strode behind the counter and disappeared through an open door into the kitchen.

Nondescript music played low in the background and Tammy sat back in her chair and turned her head to look at Katherine's customers—hopefully soon to be her own. They were old and young. Some were unmistakable tourists in their bright get-ups and flip-flops. Others Tammy recognised from the pub last night as being local residents. She smiled and said hello to the couple who caught her looking their way. Slightly embarrassed, she turned her attention to the window. Leaning over, she could see her uncle packing the ice in the cart around the remaining fish he had. Seagulls flew overhead and her uncle looked up and shuffled closer to the cart, protective of his livelihood.

Tammy fell into a daydream trance as she people-watched. Some idled by with all the time in the world, while others were more frantic. She wondered if her parents had ever sat here in the café on one of their dates, doing just as she was doing while holding hands across the table.

Katherine pulled Tammy from her daze when she placed a large oval plate and a mug down in front of her. The smell of the offering instantly made her salivate, even though Tammy hadn't really been very hungry a moment ago. Her eyes widened when she saw what Katherine had whipped up for her. It was a hearty breakfast of fluffy pancakes, crispy bacon, and scrambled eggs, served up with a mug of piping hot tea.

'Enjoy,' Katherine winked. 'We can have a chat in about thirty minutes when it goes quiet.'

'Thanks Katherine. This looks tremendous.'

As Tammy ate, she watched Katherine bantering cheerfully with customers, thinking she had a lot to learn about running a café hospitality business. She wasn't a novice when it came to running a business, but Richi had always been the face of theirs, preferring to interact with customers in their bakery shop while she stayed in the background, or kept in the kitchen doing anything but serving. If only she'd been a bit more hands-on in that area, then maybe Richi wouldn't have met and flirted with the woman who took her place in his heart.

The lump of emotion was back in her throat and Tammy had to swallow her pancake hard to get past it. She clenched her teeth together. She refused to cry—especially in the café in front of others.

When the mid-morning rush died down, Katherine finally sat down in the seat across from Tammy. 'Phew. That was a busy morning. I'm going to miss the hustle and bustle of it.'

Tammy smiled warmly at Katherine. 'Do you mind me asking why you are renting out your business? I hope you don't think I'm prying—it's just that—your business is booming at the moment.'

Katherine sighed. 'It's my mum. She's elderly and the time has come for me to move back and be there for her. She has always been fiercely independent and it will take some time for her to get used to me being there again, but it has to be done.'

'Oh, I am sorry, said Tammy earnestly. What she wouldn't give to be in the same position.

'Sadly, it's life, Tammy. You might find yourself in my shoes in the future.'

Tammy shook her head and looked out of the window towards Ben. 'Ben's the only family I have Katherine.'

Tammy felt Katherine's hand cover hers and squeeze. 'Then you're a very lucky young lady because Ben is a wonderful human being.' Katherine released Tammy's hand and patted it. 'Come on. Let's talk shop before the lunchtime rush starts.' Katherine's smile and enthusiasm were infectious. 'Let's talk about stock first. I don't know what type of eatery you plan to do, but I'll gift you everything that's left over in the café come Friday when I hand the keys over to you.'

'Friday?' Tammy's stomach did a loop-the-loop with excitement and nerves. 'Katherine nodded. 'That's *very* generous of you. Are you sure, Katherine? Uncle Ben is helping me out, so it's not a problem to buy your stock from you.

Kath held the palms of her hands up to Tammy. 'No. I insist.'

'Thank you.'

Katherine nodded. 'What do you plan to do? Are you still planning on doing hot food?'

Tammy crossed her arms on the table and leaned forward to Katherine, her enthusiasm rising to the surface. 'Well, I have an idea of turning the café into a tearoom with hot simple lunches like toasties, bacon, or vegan alternative baps and baked goods. I have a list of cakes I've already planned to do.'

'Oh, that sounds truly wonderful. I might have to drive back up here with Mum for a cream tea. She'd love that.' Katherine was fully supportive, and it was as if a weight had been lifted off Tammy's shoulders. 'I get most of my fundamental supplies from the local cash 'n' carry, but for sourcing staples like eggs, bacon, and sausages as well as organic ingredients, I recommend the local farm shop. They give me a great deal. I advise you introduce yourself to the owner to negotiate pricing.'

Using the notes app in her phone, Tammy's thumbs were going ten to the dozen, as Katherine spoke. Looking at the screen full of helpful advice from Katherine, Tammy was filled with renewed confidence. She looked up at Katherine. 'Thanks Katherine. Is the farm shop walkable from here?'

Katherine spluttered a laugh. 'Goodness no. You'd probably get trampled by cows anyway if you tried to get there by foot. Didn't you drive here, Tammy?'

She shook her head. 'I-I shared a car with...someone, but he has it now.' Saying it out loud made her sound so pathetic. 'Is there a local taxi or uber?'

Katherine pointed to the notice board. 'Mina is our local uber driver in the daytime while her children are at school. Her business card is on the board.'

The doorbell tinkled, alerting Katherine to another customer. 'No rest for the wicked eh Tammy?' She stood up as she winked at her. 'Call in anytime if you think of something else you'd like to ask me. Otherwise, we need to meet up sometime after closing so I can show you the working of the till, the oven, and whatnot.'

'Sounds like a plan,' Tammy grinned as she got to her feet, too. 'By the way. That breakfast was utterly divine. Thank you.'

Katherine smiled. 'You're welcome.'

Chapter six

Outside the café, Tammy booked the uber and then walked over to Ben. He was sitting on a small wooden stool and gave her a little wave as she approached him.

'There you are. I wondered if I'd see you before I packed up for the day.'

Tammy peered into the cart and was surprised to see there were only three fish left, although she hadn't a clue what type of fish they were. She pointed at the contents of the cart which was now mainly half melted ice. 'Busy day?'

'It sure has been. I think you're my lucky charm.' Tammy giggled. 'Have you spoken to Katherine yet about the café?'

'Yes, she's given me advice on where to get supplies. As a matter of fact, I'm waiting for an uber to take me to the farm shop to try and negotiate the continuation of the discount Katherine receives with them.'

'Ah, good thinking.'

Tammy crinkled up her nose. 'I can't actually take the credit for the idea Uncle Ben. It was Katherine's idea.'

A car pulling up at the café caught Tammy's attention as she glanced back over her shoulder. 'Jeez. That was quick. That's my uber.'

Ben looked around Tammy at the car. 'Oh, that's Mina. She only lives fifty feet away in that house there—the pink one.'

Ben pointed to a row of brightly coloured terraced houses, each one with flower boxes underneath the windows, abundant with flowers.

'Right, I'll see you later Uncle Ben. Is there anything you'd like me to get while I'm at the farm shop?'

'Can you get some lamb chops or a couple of small braising steaks? It's been ages since I had something other than fish for supper.'

'Okay.' Tammy had to quickly turn her back on her uncle to hide the grin that had erupted. Her comment was right about them only eating fish for breakfast, lunch, and supper. She reminded herself to order a supermarket food delivery—with no fish on the list.

Mina was staring at the café door waiting for her to come out, so when she tapped on the passenger window, she saw Mina jump with fright. The electric window rolled down and Mina looked up at Tammy.

'Tammy is it for the farm shop?'

'Yes. That's me. Sorry about frightening you like that. I was standing over by Ben.'

Mina looked through her window screen at Ben and waved. He waved back. Tammy opened the passenger side door and got into Mina's car.

'Aw, I love old fisherman Ben. Doesn't he have the best beard? In fact, with his woolly hat and his dungarees, he'd be the perfect model to put on the side of a tin of tuna.' Tammy's eyebrows shot up. Mina glanced her way as she turned the car around on the cobbled beachfront. 'What? You disagree?' Now Mina looked shocked.

A chuckle tickled past Tammy's tonsils. 'I don't disagree at all. I think my Uncle Ben should be on a twenty-foot tall billboard as the face behind *Young's* fish.'

Mina gasped and flung her hand to her mouth. 'Oh no. I hope you don't think I'm rude—my apologises. Me and my big mouth. I haven't offended you, have I?'

Tammy glanced at Mina's hand still on her mouth. 'No, not offended me, but I am a little frightened right now. Do you mind putting both of your hands back on that steering wheel?' she smiled brightly, showing Mina she wasn't upset.

'Sorry.' Mina quickly took hold of the steering wheel with both hands. 'I didn't even know Ben had family. I've not seen him receive one visitor in all the time I've been here, and I've lived here since I was nine.' She gasped again. 'Sorry. That came out wrong. I made it sound like you haven't been here for him, but I don't know anything about you.' Tammy could feel her forehead vein bulging again. 'Ugh, please forgive me, Tammy. I have a habit of sticking my foot in my great big mouth, but I mean well.'

Tammy gave her a smile. 'Don't worry about it. Uncle Ben's and my story is a complicated one. Maybe if we get to know each other a little better in the near future, I'll share it with you.'

'Oh. That's intriguing. You're bating me with the promise of your life story. By hinting you're staying here longer than a mere visit or a holiday, aren't you?'

Tammy just smiled and offered Mina no other information.

Ten minutes later, Mina was driving up a narrow country lane littered with animal dung. Now she knew what Katherine meant about attempting to get to the farm shop on foot. The road was clearly a thoroughfare for cows.

Mina pulled to a stop to the left of the shop. She grimaced at Tammy. 'A bit awkward, but if you want a return journey, my business card does state I still charge by the minute while I'm waiting.'

'Yes-yes, that's fine. I have no idea how long this is going to take...but don't go anywhere.'

Mina smiled and nodded like an obedient puppy.

Stepping inside the charming rustic shop filled with the scents of fresh produce, homemade scented candles, and freshly painted wooden toys. Tammy was caught off guard when she saw Pharis chatting with a young woman who, by the look of her overall, was the shopkeeper. His eyebrows lifted high when he saw her, and one corner of his mouth quirked up.

'We have got to stop meeting like this,' she said wryly. The young shopkeeper's eyes lit up in recognition.

'You must be Tammy! Pharis was just telling me about your Uncle Ben's birthday celebration in The Cheese Wedge and Pickles, and the birthday cake you made for him... He was very impressed with it, and it takes a lot to impress Pharis.'

Now it was Tammy's turn to raise her eyebrows. She looked at Pharis questioningly. Pharis shot the young girl daggers and her cheeks instantly flushed. 'I'll just go and restock the candles,' she quickly said and headed towards the back of the shop.

Tammy took a step forward, holding up her hand. 'Wait! I need to discuss buying stock with you.'

The young girl pointed to Pharis. 'Then you'd better talk with the owner.' She swiftly opened a door and disappeared through it.

Tammy's index finger stretched out and her other fingers curled under it as she pointed at Pharis. 'You... You're the owner of the farm shop?'

Pharis shrugged and grinned. 'Guilty as charged. Yes, my family and I own it.'

Tammy flushed, both embarrassed and annoyed that her business plans were dependent on Pharis.

Seeing Pharis in the farm shop standing tall and proud in his chequered shirt and denim jeans, Tammy felt more than a spark of awareness of his rugged features and athletic build. She coughed to hide her involuntary gasp when her eyes finally finished marvelling at the width of his chest and rose to meet his piercing hazel eyes. The tingle she felt was surely just irritation at his cocky attitude, she told herself.

She swallowed and then licked her lips to moisten her dry mouth. 'Then I'd like to introduce myself as the new tenant of Katherine's café. I'm taking it over next week.'

Pharis grinned wildly and crossed his burly arms across his large chest. 'Hmm. So we'll be bumping into each other quite often then?'

Tammy cleared her throat, trying to find the courage to ask for the same discount Katherine had set in place. 'Well, that depends.'

Pharis took a step closer. Is it getting hotter in here Tammy ?

hat?'

'If I can get my supplies at the same...if not, *better* deal than what Katherine has in place with you.'

Pharis huffed. 'You're as ruthless as you are pretty.'

Tammy could feel her cheeks getting hotter. She wasn't ruthless. If she was, she wouldn't have let Richi take her for everything she had after he was the one who'd done the dirty on her.

As they negotiated, his gaze kept drifting to her lips in a way that made her hair stand on end. Tammy crossed her arms tightly, willing herself not to betray any reaction. She would not be seduced by this arrogant man's attention. He was likely only interested in a challenge, and she refused to be a conquest.

His roguish grin made her bristle, even as her pulse quickened. Tammy stood her ground, fighting the long-buried urges Pharis' bold gaze awakened. She was here as a professional, not a hormonal schoolgirl. With relief, she escaped the charged air between them, grateful for the reappearance of the young shop girl. No man would disarm her so easily again.

'Is that a yes, then?'

He thrust his large, calloused hand forward. 'It's a deal.'

Her small hand became lost in his as he wrapped his brutishly strong fingers around hers to shake.

She pulled her hand free. 'Great. I'll be back later in the week with a list.' She didn't wait for a reply. She hurried out of the farm shop, feeling flustered. The cool breeze outside helped cool her cheeks and she took a moment to breathe it in before getting into Mina's car.

Mina stared at her profile. 'Hot in there, was it? Your cheeks are like beacons.' Tammy looked out of the window to avoid eye contact paranoid Mina would be able to read what just transgressed like a gypsy reading tea leaves. Mina reversed and drove slowly over a large pile of dung, making her way back down the country lane. 'Okay, am I taking you back to the café or to Ben's cottage?'

'The cottage, please.' When they were just about to pull onto the main road, Tammy hit her forehead with the heel of her hand. 'Oh no. I forgot to buy lamb chops for Ben.'

'Do you want me to turn around?'

Tammy shook her head. 'No, not to worry. I have to come back in a couple of days. I'll get some then.' Mina pulled out onto the road. 'Actually Mina, can you drop me at The Cheese Wedge and Pickles? I'll see if they will do me a couple of meals to go.'

'Sure.'

TAMMY WAVED GOODBYE to Mina. She took out her phone and checked the time. It was only 3.05 PM. Too late to order from the lunchtime menu. She would just have to come back later to buy their evening meal.

Turning around, she decided to take a stroll along the beach. She couldn't even remember the last time she had been to the seaside.

The afternoon sun warmed Tammy's shoulders as she strolled along the beach, weaving around families splashing in the surf and building elaborate sandcastles. She smiled as a little girl protested at her father as he rubbed more sun cream on the tip of her button nose. Tammy wondered if her own parents had ever brought her here as a child, building castles as the tide swept over their feet. Had her father chased her in the frothy surf? Had her mother swept her hair up into a ponytail to keep her unruly curls from her eyes as she played in the waves? But any memories from before their death were lost, swept away like footprints on these shifting sands.

Wandering farther down the shoreline, Tammy spotted a church steeple in the distance. Drawn by curiosity, she left the beach and wandered through the adjoining cemetery, brushing her fingers over worn gravestones as she tried to decipher the faded names. She squinted her eyes as she tried to read the weathered inscriptions, wondering if she had any relatives resting here, their histories now etched in eroded stone.

Approaching the picturesque church, Tammy saw that the large wooden door stood open. She hesitated briefly, then stepped inside, escaping the cemetery's melancholy air. The sanctuary was deliciously cold after the heat outside and it was empty save for a priest tidying up the front pews. He turned with a warm smile as Tammy's footsteps echoed off the vaulted ceiling.

'Welcome!' he called. 'I'm Reverend Townsend. Are you visiting our lovely seaside town?'

'Erm yes and no.' Tammy replied, returning his smile tentatively. 'I'm Tammy Vaugh, Ben Hickman's niece.'

The Reverend's eyes lit up in recognition. 'Of course! Ben mentioned in passing that you were coming. He's a wonderful man. Yes and no is a very odd answer,' he chuckled.

Tammy walked closer as she explained. 'My visit has somehow turned into a much longer stay.' She lifted her arms from her sides and then dropped them down again. 'I'm about to take over Katherine's café. It was a spur of the moment decision after my circumstances changed prior to my visit here.'

The Reverend clasped his hands in delight. 'What wonderful news! The Lord does indeed work in mysterious ways. My prayers have been answered.' His chuckle was light-hearted, his eyes crinkling at the corners.

Swept up in his enthusiasm, Tammy found herself confessing more about her new endeavour. 'I'll be keeping most of Katherine's menu, but I'll be expanding on it to include more baked goods come lunchtime. I'm a baker by trade,' she concluded.

'So it will be less of a café and more of a tearoom?'

Tammy tilted her head to the side. 'I guess it will.'

'Well, my dear, it sounds like you'll be running Tammy's Tearoom to me!' Reverend Townsend declared.

Tammy's pulse quickened at the suggestion. She hadn't even thought about changing the name of the business. Her own tearoom! 'Oh Reverend. I think you've found the perfect name for my business.' She hesitated. 'It's a shame it will have to wait to change it. I don't have the budget for a new sign yet.'

The Reverend merely smiled serenely. 'Ask and it shall be given. Seek and ye shall find. Knock and it shall be opened unto you.' I will pray for everything to work out splendidly. His calm confidence was contagious.

At that moment, Tammy was struck by inspiration. 'Reverend,' she began tentatively, 'is there any chance I was christened at this church? I don't have any records, but since my uncle has been here so long...' she trailed off hopefully.

The Reverend's eyes crinkled again as he regarded her. 'As a matter of fact, you were. I performed the ceremony myself.'

Seeing Tammy's mouth drop open, he continued, 'And I also officiated your parents' wedding right here in this sanctuary.' Overwhelmed with emotion, Tammy sank slowly into a pew. 'I'll go and fetch the old church record books.' He hurried away.

Tammy's eyes looked around, her eyes finding a christening font in a corner. Her chest fluttered. *I was christened here*, she thought to herself. Her eyes went to the altar. *And my parents were married there*. She had found out more in the last twenty-four hours about her parents and her own life than she'd known in twenty-seven years alive.

The Reverend came out of a door carrying two large books. He placed them on her lap and opened the top book to a page with a bookmark peeping out. On faded parchment were two minuscule baby footprints. Tammy gasped.

'Those are your feet. Your mother insisted on having prints of them.' He chuckled, 'I remember how unimpressed I'd been when she'd dipped your feet in special ink and then placed them on the page. It was most unorthodox, but I couldn't protest because they'd been so lovely.' Tammy traced her finger around the edge of them. The Reverend lifted the christening ledger off her lap and opened the book beneath it. He pointed to unfamiliar loopy black scrawls. 'Those are your parent's signatures.'

Tammy reverently brushed her fingers over the records, tracing each letter. Tears threatened to spill, and she lifted her head back for fear they would drop onto the page and blur the ink. She had no memories of her parents, just one faded old photo, no connections to who they were or the love they shared. Yet here in her hands, at last, was real, tangible proof of the family she had lost.

'They were the first couple I ever married.' The Reverend's voice was soothing as he settled beside her. 'Apparently, your mother grew up attending this church, and your father moved to town a few years before they met. It was a beautiful ceremony...'

As he recounted details, Tammy pictured her parents standing hand in hand at the altar, gazing lovingly into each other's eyes as they exchanged vows. In her mind, she could see her mother walking down the aisle in a simple lace gown, face glowing beneath her veil. And her father, dashing and nervous in his smart suit, waiting for his bride with tears in his eyes.

The Reverend's lilting voice faded into the background as Tammy lost herself in daydreams—her father tossing baby Tammy into the air as she giggled uncontrollably, her mother singing sweet lullabies as she rocked Tammy to sleep. They were only fantasies, and yet so real Tammy could nearly reach out and touch them.

When Reverend Townsend gently offered Tammy his handkerchief, she realised her cheeks were wet with silent tears. She glanced down to see several dark drops had fallen on her mother's signature. 'I'm so sorry,' she gasped, dabbing at the blotted ink.

But the Reverend clasped her hand warmly. 'Don't be, my dear. Your parents would be happy their daughter has finally come home.' His words only brought fresh tears, but Tammy's spirit felt lighter than it had in years.

After composing herself, Tammy embraced the kindly Reverend, thanking him profusely for connecting her with the history she feared was lost. As they said goodbye at the door, a light breeze swept through the cemetery, carrying the faint sound of laughter on it. Tammy stood transfixed, letting the wind caress her tear-streaked cheeks.

Somehow, standing in the shadow of the church that had joined and blessed her family, she sensed her parents' presence like never before. Their love surrounded her, enveloping her in a brief sensation of warmth and light.

As Tammy walked slowly back down the beach, her mind replayed each discovered treasure—her baby footprints, her parents' signatures, the christening and wedding ceremonies. She may have no photos or memories of them, but suddenly the blanks of her past were starting to fill with colour and shape. The foundations of who she was and where she came from felt more solid, like sun-warmed sand moulding firmly beneath her feet.

One thing was clear, life in her new seaside town was turning out to be undoubtedly more interesting the longer she was here.

Act two – Chapter seven

'I can't believe you've only been here for five days. It feels as though you've always been here with me.'

Tammy looked up from the list she was preparing and smiled at her Uncle Ben. 'Is that a good thing or a bad one?'

Ben pulled on his scraggy grey beard as he laughed. 'Good. I didn't realise how quiet and empty this house was until you arrived.'

She looked around the kitchen and realised she'd taken over somewhat. There were potted plants in the window, a new colourful tea towel draped over the handle of the cooker, and three brand new matching pots on the work surface for coffee, tea, and sugar.

'Sorry Uncle Ben. These were extra things I bought for the tearoom, but I changed my mind about them in the end.'

'I'm not complaining my dear. You've breathed life into the bones of this old house.' Ben's words meant a lot to her. 'What are your plans for today?' he asked.

'I'm making a list of the last-minute things I need to buy and do. I'm nervous Uncle Ben. I've never run a business venture alone before. I did all this with Richi when I decided to break free of my job to become self-employed.'

'You'll be fine. Stop fretting. I'm here to help if you need me.'

'Thank you, Uncle Ben.' Tammy got to her feet. 'I'm off down the town. Is there anything you want me to get whilst I'm out?'

Ben chuckled. 'Depends. Will this be another lamb chop tuned into a Chinese takeout incident? I don't know if I can take that much excitement again.'

Tammy chuckled. 'I made it up to you two days later, didn't I? I got lamb chop and braising steak and cooked you a wonderful meaty supper.'

'That you did.' Ben nodded in agreement. 'No. I don't need anything this time thank you.'

Tammy hugged him and shoved the shopping list into her bag. 'Okay...well, I'm off. I'll see you later, Uncle Ben.'

The morning sun peeked through wispy clouds as Tammy made her way down Seagull Bay's cobblestone main street. Today was dedicated to gathering supplies and decor to bring her new tearoom to life. She wanted to create a warm, welcoming ambiance for visitors to enjoy. Not that there was anything wrong with Katherine's current style, it was just that she wanted to make it her own. Richi had had far too much influence on the way their bakery had been decorated and styled. This time, it was all going to be her choice.

Her first stop was the local home goods store: Bell, Book, and Table. Pushing open the weathered green door, Tammy was greeted by the cheerful tinkling of a bell and the aroma of lavender candles. The shop was small, but it was jammed full. Tammy picked up a basket and then took her time wandering the few aisles, running her fingers over the embroidered table linens and handmade pottery. She chose plastic gingham blue check tablecloths. They weren't exactly the look she was going for, but she had a limited budget, and at least they would match the window dressings.

By the time she left the small quaint shop, with bagfuls of tablecloths, mini ceramic vases to house the fresh flowers she intended to put on every table, and assorted scented candles, her wallet was significantly lighter. But she couldn't resist the charming tea towels printed with seashells, seagulls, and nautical motifs. They perfectly captured the essence of her coastal town and they reminded her of her uncle.

Next was the frame shop, where Tammy had spotted several prints of seascapes and lighthouses in the window when she'd passed by in Mina's car on the way to the farm shop. In her mind's eye she had already chosen the places on the tearoom wall they'd adorn. She imagined guests gazing at them while sipping tea and then turning their heads to watch the real ocean just outside.

At the register, the owner Mrs. Klein recognised her. 'You're Tammy aren't you?' Tammy's eyes widened and she nodded. 'I've seen you walking about this week, and someone pointed you out as the lady who will be taking over Katherine's café and opening it up as a tearoom,' she said brightly. 'I'm guessing these prints are to be used for your new décor, because Ben has never stepped inside this place, let alone bought anything new for his cottage.'

Tammy smiled. News certainly travelled fast around here. 'Yes, they are, and my Uncle Ben's house doesn't need anything new. It's perfect as it is.'

The owner's face blanched. 'Oh, I didn't mean anything by what I said.'

Tammy smiled. 'I know.' She leaned in close and lowered her voice. 'It is kind of stuck in the fifties, but don't tell him I said that.' She finished with a wink.'

The storekeeper giggled with relief. 'I won't... Here, let me get the door for you.'

'Thank you and be sure to come and check out the art once it's hung in the tearoom.'

'I will.'

Tammy left the shop smiling. There was one guaranteed customer. She was loaded down with bags practically bursting at the seams and now with framed prints under each arm as well.

She slowly made her way back up the street, trying her best to dodge the tourists. Rounding a corner, she stumbled slightly under the weight of her purchases, then felt someone's strong grip on her waist. Once she was righted, the hands left her and grasped several of the bags from her overloaded arms.

'Here, let me help you with those.' She instantly recognised the smoky voice before the man it belonged to came into view, offering her a kind smile.

Tammy hated to admit it, but she could have kissed him right at that moment. 'Declan! You're a lifesaver,' Tammy sighed with relief, adjusting her grip on the remaining bags. They continued to walk side by side.

'So the rumour is true then?' he asked.

Tammy bristled slightly, thinking how rumours spread so fast in such a small town. 'If by rumour you mean the common knowledge that *I am* taking over Katherine's café, then yes, it's true,' she replied.

Declan chuckled at her thinly veiled irritation. 'My apologies. I only meant I hadn't heard it *confirmed* from the source yet, so I didn't know if it was true.' His easy grin and light tone smoothed Tammy's ruffled feathers. 'Is that where we're heading? For the café? It will be shut now. Katherine will be home.'

'Not to worry. I have a set of keys.'

'Ah ha. Of course you do.' He grinned impishly at Tammy and it actually made Tammy's tummy flutter. 'Are you looking to hire any extra staff yet?'

Shaking her head, Tammy replied, 'Not yet. I need to get on my feet first before I can manage employees. Plus, I need to make sure I can pay my own wages before I pay anyone else's. But I'll spread the word when I'm ready.' She turned and looked at Declan's profile. He appeared to be frowning or deep in thought. 'Why? Do you know of anyone who's in need of work?' He shook his head, but Tammy had an inkling he was enquiring for himself.

They soon arrived at the cafe, and Tammy unlocked the door, flipping on the light in the dwindling light of the day. Declan followed her inside, setting the shopping bags atop the nearest table.

As Tammy began unpacking her purchases, Declan glanced around. Tammy followed his eyes, which noted the unopened cans of paint at the corner of the room which Tammy had brought the day before from Old Po's hardware shop. 'Need an extra hand getting this place decorated? I'm a dab hand. I've recently decorated my place throughout.'

Tammy hesitated. Though she could use the help, working closely with Declan might fan the sparks she felt between them. And after her last relationship disaster, romance was off the table for the foreseeable future.

Still, the task was too big to tackle alone in the short time she had. Pushing aside her reservations, she gave Declan a grateful nod. 'Actually, that would be great. I want to freshen up the look before opening day.'

'Which is?'

'On Monday. Katherine has already closed the café for a couple of days. Didn't you see the sign in the window? Katherine put it up today.'

Declan licked his lips. 'Actually, I didn't. I was too distracted looking at something else when we rocked up here.'

Tammy blinked at his statement—she knew exactly what he meant. She had felt his eyes burning into her as she'd fumbled with the lock because it had been her first time opening up, but she'd tactfully ignored it.

'I'm starting the painting tonight, but don't you have to work at the pub?'

'Actually, lucky for you, it's my night off. Let me just pop home to change into some old clothes and see to my dog, and then we can make a start.'

'You have a pet? Isn't there anyone to look after it whilst you are at work?'

'Fernando does okay. I pop back whenever I get a break and let him out for five minutes.'

'Oh okay. Great name for a big dog, by the way.'

Declan nodded in agreement. 'Thanks.'

'Do you live far?'

Declan grinned and pointed up at the ceiling. Seeing the confusion on Tammy's face, he explained. 'I live right upstairs in the flat above the cafe. Just a stone's throw from The Cheese Wedge and Pickles. It's quite convenient, isn't it?' Tammy gasped and followed him to the door. 'I won't be long.'

Declan lived above her new business. She'd see him whether she wanted to or not. She watched him head outside and busied herself unpacking her new decor.

She didn't hear the knock at first over the crinkling of the shopping bags. The second, more forceful rap on the door finally got her attention. Expecting Declan's return, Tammy was surprised when she looked up to see Pharis sauntering in.

'Pharis! I wasn't expecting you...' she began, but he cut her off.

'Got a little surprise out back for you,' he announced with a mysterious grin, beckoning her to follow him as he left the café. Curiosity piqued; Tammy followed him out the door to the cobbled road leading down to a small parking area by the beachfront. There, on the back of a pickup truck, was a large painted wooden sign reading 'Tammy's Tearoom' in swirling pastel letters.

Tammy's jaw dropped. 'Oh my goodness! What...how?' she stammered.

Pharis chuckled at her shocked expression. 'Remember how the reverend offered to pray for help to get a new sign for you? Well, his prayers came my way. I had some free time this week, so I figured, why not lend a hand? I make and paint all the toys we sell in the farm shop, so this was a doddle.'

Overcome with gratitude, Tammy threw her arms around Pharis in an exuberant hug. 'You wonderful man! How can I ever repay you for this kindness?' Tammy's reaction had come naturally. Before Richi did the dirty on her, she was a very

tactile person. It had only been the past six months that she'd
shied away from hugs.

Pharis looked a bit pink as they parted. 'Don't mention it.
Consider it a welcome gift from the community of Seagull Bay
to you.'

Just then, Declan appeared with a large St Bernard on a
lead. He cleared his throat loudly. Tammy took a quick step
back from Pharis, feeling suddenly self-conscious. Both men
eyed each other coolly before Declan broke the silence.

'There you are. Sorry it took me longer than a minute. I
couldn't find my painting clothes.' Declan dipped his head at
Pharis. 'Evening Pharis. Did I hear you say the sign is a gift from
the Seagull Bay community? I didn't hear about the project, or
I would have offered my help.' Though he kept his tone light,
Tammy sensed tension crackling in the air between the two of
them.

'Like I said, it's a gift from the Seagull Bay community. You
only moved here a few months ago, so...'

Keen to diffuse the tension, Tammy quickly cut off Pharis's
reply. 'It's amazing, whoever it came from. Are you putting it
up tonight? Only the daylight is quickly dwindling.'

Pharis shook his head. 'No. I'll leave it here and come back
tomorrow with my tools. Will you be here?'

'All day,' Tammy replied brightly.

'Great.' He looked across to Declan. 'Can you help me
unload it?'

'Are you sure I'm up to the job? In your eyes. I'm not
exactly a Seagull Bay resident, now am I?'

Pharis opened his mouth to answer, but Tammy stepped in front of him and offered her hand for the leash. 'I'll hold Fernando for you. Is he friendly?'

Pharis glanced Tammy's way. 'Some people from out of town are useful—others aren't.' He looked back at Declan. 'We'll see what category you fall into. Shall we?'

Tammy huffed. She was an out-of-towner, and she was taking over the café. She'd like to know what Pharis' thoughts on her were. She'd give him a piece of her mind, too. Taking hold of the lead, she led the St Bernard over to the café where there was a bowl of water outside for customers' pets. 'Come on Fernando. There's too much hot air blowing around here. Let's go get you a drink.'

Fernando wagged his bushy tail happily, none the wiser about the friction between his owner and another man, as Tammy led him over to the water bowl. As the dog drank, Tammy watched Declan and Pharis get the large wooden sign off the truck, with Pharis dishing out orders about how Declan should grab the sign. Neither one looked impressed with the other.

As they worked together, Tammy couldn't help but admire them both. They were like chalk and cheese in looks. Declan was pale for this time of year with short, almost black hair and bright blue eyes, while Pharis had a dark Mediterranean look about him, as if his ancestry originated from sunnier climates.

Tammy shook her head and silently scolded herself. 'You're off men Tammy—remember?'

When the sign was resting against the café's frontage, Pharis dipped his head at Declan. 'Thanks.'

'No problem,' replied Declan. 'I'll give you a hand putting it up tomorrow. I'll look out for your truck. I live right above the café.'

Tammy noticed how Pharis stiffened when he heard the news. He looked at the cafe and then up to the widows above it. Nodding once as his reply, he turned his back on Declan and strode back to his truck to retrieve a length of folded tarp. Walking briskly back to the sign, he unwrapped the tarp and stretched it across it.

Declan reclaimed the leash from Tammy while Pharis fussed with the tarp. 'I'll take Fernando back upstairs, then I'll help you with that painting.'

'I'll stop and help if you like,' Pharis quickly added from behind Declan.

Tammy was speechless, and before she could answer, Declan answered for her. 'Too many chefs spoil the broth.'

Pharis ignored Declan and looked at Tammy with raised eyebrows, waiting for her confirmation of Declan's statement.

She didn't think she could paint the café with the ongoing tension between Pharis and Declan. 'No. It's fine, really. You've done more than enough to help me. I'm ever so grateful for what you've done. Your first few visits to Tammy's Tearoom will be on the house,' she chuckled, hoping her gesture would appease him after turning down his offer to help with the decorating.

'Okay. I'll get off then. I'll see you first thing.'

'I'll have freshly brewed coffee waiting for you.'

Tammy watched him climb into his truck. He flashed her a smile before pulling away. She sighed. Was she a magnet for man trouble? Turning around, she walked slowly back into the café, glancing at the covered sign with a grin on the way. Her stomach fluttered with excitement. In just a few days, she would have her own tearoom, with no man to ruin her new business venture this time. As for Decan and Pharis, she wouldn't have time for petty posturing from either man.

Over the next couple of hours, Declan and Tammy completely transformed the café's interior. Soft yellow paint refreshed the walls, while Tammy's new decorations she'd bought added oceanfront charm.

By late evening, sore muscles and growling stomachs signalled a good stopping point. Standing back to admire their work, Tammy was elated. 'It's even better than I imagined! We are miracle workers.'

Declan gave a mock bow. 'My pleasure to lend my expert painting skills to such a lovely locale.'

Tammy pooh-poohed him away with the flick of her hand. 'I'm no more a local than you are by the sounds of things.'

Declan grinned. 'Us outsiders should stick together. How about I rustle up some supper for us?'

Tammy froze at the suggestion. Although her heart was screaming yes, her head knew it was definitely *not* a good idea. 'Thank you for the offer, but I really need to get back to my uncle. Anyway, it's me who should be offering you a meal for all your hard work.'

'Is that an offer for a date?' his wonky grin stirred something inside Tammy.

'No,' she shook her head a little too vigorously, making the grin fall from Declan's mouth. 'I meant, I can offer you a free meal when I'm up and running—*a few free meals*,' she quickly added.

'Okay...great.' Declan walked backward to the door. 'I'll see you in the morning when I help Pharis with your new sign.'

Tammy nodded and raised her hand. 'Okay...thanks again.'

Declan nodded and exited the café and Tammy was left alone with her thoughts. She thought making a fresh start in Seagull Bay was just the thing to wash Richi out of her system, but it appeared she had jumped out of the frying pan into the fire.

Chapter eight

Tammy was up at the crack of dawn with her uncle. He looked shocked to see her when she appeared in the kitchen as he was washing up his mug before leaving to claim the best fish from the early returning fishermen.

'Goodness me. I expected you to lay in bed longer today after all your hard work decorating the café yesterday.'

Tammy hugged her uncle and then lit the gas ring on the hob and placed the kettle onto it. Her uncle always made sure he left fresh water in the kettle for her before he left in the mornings. He was so thoughtful, and the only man Tammy needed or *wanted* in her life.

'Pharis is coming to put my new sign up. He's a farm lad, so I'm expecting his mornings to be in the same time zone as yours uncle—very early.' Ben chuckled. 'And then I need to go and see Katherine to finalise things.'

'Give her my regards,' Ben grinned, the crinkles around his eyes deepening, making him appear all the more endearing to Tammy.

'I will.' Ben made for the door that led into the lean-to hut. 'Uncle Ben, I won't be home for supper tonight. I want to start baking to stock up for Monday's grand opening.'

'Okay lass, but don't work too hard and go wearing yourself out.'

Tammy's chest swelled with love. 'I won't.'

AS TAMMY HEADED DOWN the hill to the town, she admired the view she now called home. The sun was just rising over the sea on the horizon, casting a magical glow over everything its rays touched.

The windowpanes of every house she passed on each side of the street reflected the warm orangey glow of the sun, and Tammy felt like she was experiencing the most perfect morning ever.

Her phone vibrated in her back pocket and she pulled it out to check her messages.

Tammy Vaughn, I haven't heard a word from you in days. I tried calling you, but your answering machine kicked in, so I had to leave a message. But guess what? You never got back to me. Please just let me know you're okay.

From your VERY worried friend.

Sucking in a gasp, Tammy's hand flew up to her mouth. She'd been in Seagull Bay nearly a week and she hadn't once thought to text or call Evelyn. It was a little early to be having a full-blown conversation, as some people might still be tucked up in bed. The last thing they wanted to hear was her cockney accent acting as an alarm clock.

She opted to text back.

Morning Evelyn.

I'm so sorry. It's been a whirlwind here. My uncle is absolutely adorable. Seagull Bay is exquisite, and I'm about to open my own tearoom. There's too much to tell you in a

**text, so I'll call you this evening. Must go, I'm meeting two
local men who are going to hang my sign.**

Pocketing her phone, Tammy practically skipped the rest
of the way down the hill with her phone frantically vibrating,
alerting her of many more messages being received and
reminding her of how little patience Evelyn had.

Turning the corner at the bottom of the hill, Tammy's pace
picked up as she neared the beachfront. Today was the first
official day of her taking over Katherine's café. In two days'
time, it would be re-opened as Tammy's Tearoom. Her heart
felt like it skipped a beat.

The shop came into view and her breath caught in her
throat. This was far more exciting than when she'd opened the
bakery with Richi. She surmised it was because this time it was
all her own.

A light flicked on in the window above the café, drawing
Tammy's eyes. Declan's unmistakable form came into view and
this time, her tummy clenched. He didn't see her; he was
looking out at the sunrise. The same orangey glow lit up his
handsome face, making his chiselled jaw appear even sharper.
Tammy's feet came to an involuntary stop as she ogled him.

She suddenly came to her senses. 'What are you doing,
Tammy? You look like a peeping Tom,' she said aloud to herself.

Declan's head turned her way, catching her off guard. A
weird smile splayed on her mouth, and she raised her hand and
waved. He waved back, then he disappeared from the window
and the light turned off in the room.

Tammy carried on into the café. She opened up and the
smell of fresh paint made her heart stutter. It was a reminder
of new beginnings. She went straight into the kitchen to brew

some coffee, as promised to Pharis. The kitchen looked pristine. Katherine was an angel walking in human clothing. Tammy wondered how she had become so lucky after what had happened to her with Richi.

'Good morning. You're here early.'

Tammy jumped, startled by Declan's voice. She thought she'd locked the door behind her. She spun around to look up into piercing blue eyes fringed with thick black lashes.

'My goodness you startled me.' He grinned back mischievously. 'Yes, I am. I need to make a start on the baked goods. Some pastries and cake mixtures can be frozen. The more I make now, the less I have to worry about running out of stock mid-week and then fretting about making more.'

'Very wise. Be prepared for the unexpected.'

'Exactly.'

'I'd offer to help, but I've got my dirty work clothes on ready to help Pharis.'

Tammy shook her head. 'No. Really, it's fine. I never expected you to. I'm just grateful for the help yesterday and again today, with you offering to help Pharis. You've both been very kind. Do you know each other well?'

Declan shook his head. 'Not really. As Pharis alluded to yesterday, I'm not from Seagull Bay. I was hired by Pippa just over three months ago, and then shortly after, I was lucky enough to rent the flat upstairs from Katherine.'

'What brought you to reside permanently in Seagull Bay?' Tammy hated herself for being curious. She was supposed to be limiting her interactions with men, not increasing them.

'Ah... there were a few reasons. Mainly, I was fed up with sleeping on my friend's couch after my business failed, which ultimately led to the break-down of my relationship too.'

Tammy's mouth had involuntarily dropped open. Declan's circumstances couldn't be any closer to hers if they tried.

'Is that the promised fresh coffee I can smell?' Pharis stepped into the café with a grin that faltered when he saw Declan. 'You weren't joking about helping then? I thought you chef people didn't like getting your hands dirty outside the kitchen?'

Tammy looked from one handsome face to the other. She needed to diffuse the rivalry before it even started today. 'Yes, the coffee's made and if you both do a good job and work together safely, I'll even buy you a pint at lunchtime.'

Pharis clapped his hands together and the noise echoed. 'That's the only motivator I need. Okay. Coffee and brawn.' He took a step forward and slapped his large hand down on Declan's shoulder. 'What do you say, Declan?'

'I got the brawn, but I also need the coffee.'

Pharis' meaty laugh echoed louder than his thundering clap had. He looked at Tammy. 'A bacon butty wouldn't go amiss either.'

Tammy nodded and looked at Declan with her eyebrows raised. 'Declan?'

He gave her a cheeky wink. 'Brown sauce on mine and don't butter the bread.' Tammy huffed with a grin at his cheek.

'I'll take mine any way it comes.'

'A non-fussy customer—my favourite kind.'

Pharis's grin stretched from ear to ear as he looked at Declan, obviously pleased he'd scored points in round one.

Tammy giggled and turned on her heels, heading into the kitchen.

As she fried the bacon, Tammy smiled to herself. This was good. Pharis and Declan were merely her new friends—nothing more. She could throw carefree banter around like this all day long. She supposed it was just an added bonus they were eye candy.

She plated their butties and added them to the tray with their mugs of coffee, then carried the tray from the kitchen, through the shop and outside.

The men were standing about twenty feet back, side-by-side with their arms folded across their chests, looking up at the old sign with their heads leaned into each other as they discussed the best way to get the old sign down and the new one up. Tammy drank in the sight. It was almost as good as the sea view stretched out behind them.

'Breakfast is served.' They held their thumbs up but made no attempt to move. Instead, they continued to talk and point up at the sign. 'I'll leave it here, shall I?' The thumbs were up again. Tammy felt a little annoyed by the lack of attention. She had put her heart and soul into making her first meal in her new business and she'd hoped to have some acknowledgement for it at least.

'Oh. Are you open? I thought the café was closed until Monday.'

A small voice from behind startled Tammy, and she spun around to see a postman.

'Oh. Erm. Well, not officially. I made breakfast for the workers.' She pointed over at Declan and Pharis who at that moment in time did not look as if they were working.

'I'm a worker...and a very hungry one at that.'

The postman's eyes twinkled as he held his stomach and laughed. Tammy chuckled along with him. 'I-I suppose I could knock you something up. I have bacon and sausage cooked. I could rustle up a sandwich for you.'

'Any chance of a soft-yolk egg on there, too?'

Tammy dipped her head to the side with a grin. 'If you don't ask you don't get. Of course. Any sauce?'

He chuckled and shook his head. 'Exactly. No to the sauce, thank you.'

'Alright then, one sausage, egg, and bacon butty to go? I'll be two minutes.' She disappeared into the shop, returning a few minutes later with a paper bag and a paper napkin. She handed them both to him. 'For any spillages from your yolk.'

'Thanks. That's exactly what the doctor ordered,' he replied with a grin, accepting the sandwich with gratitude. 'You're a lifesaver.' He handed her a five-pound note. 'Keep the change.'

Tammy shook her head. 'No. I don't want paying, it's on the house.'

'I insist, and I'll put the word about how you made me a sandwich when you were closed.'

'I really appreciate that. Thank you. Enjoy, and have a great day!' Tammy gave him a warm smile and the postman tipped an imaginary hat and went on his way.

With another breakfast served, Tammy decided it was time to get to work on her cakes for the grand opening. She stepped back into the cafe and headed straight for the kitchen, mentally preparing for a day of baking.

Hours passed by in a flurry of mixing, measuring, and baking. The kitchen was filled with the heavenly scents of vanilla, chocolate, and freshly baked goodies. Tammy hummed as she baked, feeling a sense of accomplishment as trays of beautifully crafted cakes filled her kitchen counters. It was all coming together.

Just as she was putting the finishing touches on a batch of cupcakes, a cheerful knock sounded on the kitchen door. Tammy wiped her hands on her apron and went to answer it. It was Pharis and Declan, both with beaming smiles and mischief in their eyes.

'Ready to see my masterpiece?' Pharis asked with a grin.

Tammy's heart raced with excitement. She nodded keenly and took off her apron, hanging it on the back of the kitchen door before following them outside. The beachfront was now a hum-drum of activity and Tammy could see the beach beyond it had almost filled to capacity. The early afternoon sun cast a warm glow over the scene, making it picture-perfect. As she joined Pharis and Declan in front of the café, Pharis held his hands in front of her eyes. 'Ready?'

'Yes.' Her heart was going ten to the dozen.

'Ta-da!' Pharis announced theatrically, his hand dropping and then sweeping toward the sign. Tammy looked up, and her breath caught in her throat. There it was the sign that proudly proclaimed, 'Tammy's Tearoom.' It could no longer be referred to as a café. The font was elegant and inviting, a perfect reflection of the cosy haven she had worked so hard to create.

Tammy's eyes welled up with tears of joy. 'It-it's beautiful,' she whispered, her voice trembling with emotion.

Declan grinned at her, his eyes holding a mixture of pride and admiration. 'You did it, Tammy. This is all yours.'

Pharis nudged her playfully. 'You better get used to seeing your name up there because Seagull Bay is going to love your tearoom.'

Tammy blinked away the tears. 'Oh, I really hope so.' Overcome with emotion, she wrapped her arms around both of them in a tight hug. 'Thank you both for working so hard when you barely know me. You don't know how much I appreciate it.'

Pharis patted her back gently. 'It's been our pleasure.'

Declan pulled away slightly and looked down at her with a soft smile. 'We're glad to be here at the beginning with you in your journey to success.'

As the three of them stood there, basking in the moment, Tammy felt a sense of camaraderie and support that she hadn't experienced in a long time. Richi had been her boyfriend and her business partner, but she'd never felt as connected as she did right now. It was as if she had found her place in Seagull Bay, surrounded by friends who genuinely cared about her and her dreams.

'So,' Pharis said, breaking the silence, 'are we celebrating this moment with that promised pint?'

Tammy's eyes lit up. 'Absolutely! But first, let me just lock up the cafe.' She was buzzing. It appeared the two men worked surprisingly well together after all. Their competitiveness now history replaced with camaraderie.

With the cafe secure, they walked down the beachfront together, the sun's rays warming their backs. Declan led the way into The Cheese Wedge and Pickles.

Oliver was pulling a pint, and he lifted his chin in acknowledgement. 'Good afternoon to the workers. I saw you struggling and falling out when I took Ginger and Jess for a walk along the beach earlier. Glad to see you've made up.'

Declan lifted his finger to his lips. 'Shhh. We didn't want Tammy to know that part.'

They burst into fits of laughter.

They found a corner booth and settled in, each with a pint of beer in front of them. The conversation flowed effortlessly, filled with laughter and anecdotes. Tammy was grateful for these moments of genuine connection and lightheartedness after six months of emotional misery.

Ordering lunch, they moved out of the lively pub onto its patio, cold beers in hand, looking out at the shimmering sea. A few other patrons waved in greeting, welcoming Tammy to town. She was touched by the friendly sense of community.

Looking from one to the other, Tammy smiled. 'Truly, I can't thank you enough for all your help,' she said, raising her glass. 'I'd never have got my own sign, let alone got it fitted so quickly, without you two.'

'Anything to pitch in for the newest addition to our little community,' Pharis replied. Declan nodded in agreement, adding, 'Folks around here are always eager to help a neighbour in need.'

The afternoon sun began to dip below the horizon, casting a warm orange glow over the pub, Tammy raised her glass. 'To new beginnings, to friendship, and to Tammy's Tearoom.'

Pharis and Declan clinked their glasses against hers, and the sound resonated with a promise of the adventures that awaited them in Seagull Bay.

As Tammy chatted with them, she thought to herself that these two handsome men were shaping up to be good friends, regardless of her mixed-up feelings about men. With their generosity and shared love for the town, she mused contentedly that Seagull Bay was already starting to feel like home.

After a hearty fish and chip meal courtesy of a grateful Tammy, they parted ways outside the pub. Declan headed for his flat as Pharis climbed into his rumbling pickup. Alone, Tammy took a moment to look around her at the seafront, at the colourful houses and shops edging Seagull Bay. It was postcard-perfect, with the rays of the setting sun casting a magical aura over everything it touched.

She wandered slowly back to her tearoom, smiling at her new sign above the window. She let herself in, gazing around at the cosy, welcoming space and sat down to drink it all in. Yes, she decided, sinking happily into one of the cushioned chairs. This was exactly where she was meant to be.

She must have dozed off because she was awakened by a gentle tapping. She opened her eyes and saw her Uncle Ben's nose squashed against a window; his hands cupped around his face as he peered in at her.

Blinking away her sleepiness, she jumped to her feet and rushed to unlock the door. 'Uncle Ben. Are you okay?'

'I was going to ask you the same thing, lass. I thought you were going to see Katherine today?'

'I am Uncle Ben...Why, what time is it?'

'Half-past five. I'm sure she said she was leaving at six-thirty after the rush-hour traffic calmed down.'

Tammy's hands flew up to her cheeks. 'Oh my goodness. That pint of beer must have made me sleepy. I'd show you the new décor, but I must catch Katherine.'

'Don't worry about me. I'll see it at your grand opening.' He leaned forward and kissed her cheek. 'Don't forget to lock up. I'll see you later.' He turned around and walked off. Tammy watched him for a moment thankful he was in her life, before rushing into the kitchen to check everything was turned off. Then she switched off the lights, locked up, and headed for Katherine's house.

Chapter nine

The walk to Katherine's house felt surreal. Tammy was still feeling the sluggish aftereffects from her nap. Seagull Bay didn't offer much space for its residents. Their houses were small and the garden space limited, but they were truly blessed to live in a picturesque place like this with a beautiful beach a stone's throw away. She guessed it was a small price to pay to live in paradise.

Using the walking choice on Google maps, Tammy admired each home she passed as she walked the warren of narrow streets to get to Katherine's address, marvelling at the fact there was not one house that wasn't colourful in some way or other. If they weren't painted a wonderful pastel pink, sorbet lemon, Buckingham green or Aztec blue, there were window boxes abundant with vibrant flowers to add colour, or knitted bunting bearing intriguing pictures hanging on frontages. Tammy sighed with contentment. She really was living the dream here in Seagull Bay.

Google maps stopped her outside a baby-pink house that had both flower boxes and bunting. Tammy grinned. The exterior of Katherine's house was a true reflection of the wonderful person Tammy had grown to know in the short time she'd been here.

She lifted the brass pug knocker, its extended tongue hitting the brass plate attached to the door, and rapped it lightly. Tammy smile grew when she heard Katherine's sing-song reply.

'*Coming*!' The door opened and Katherine's kind eyes twinkled. 'I wondered when you'd get here, Tammy. I was just considering walking up to Ben's house. But in all honesty, I don't think I have the energy. I haven't stopped since the crack of dawn.' She ushered Tammy inside. 'Go through that door into the lounge. You're in luck. I just brewed a pot of tea.'

'I'm so sorry if I've kept you waiting, Katherine. I can't lie to you. I zonked out for an hour after a lunchtime beer with Pharis and Declan.'

Katherine tittered as she made her way into the kitchen, shaking her head. Tammy watched her, feeling even guiltier, before heading through the door Katherine pointed out.

Inside the house was no different from outside. Lilac floral wallpaper adorned the walls of the lounge. Tammy eyes took in the cosy scene, looking where to sit. There was just an armchair or a two-seater oversized couch filled to the brim with cushions of all shapes and sizes. Each one embroidered with a scenic photo or a picture of an animal.

The armchair had a notepad with a pen balancing on the arm, undoubtedly Katherine's chair, so Tammy opted for the mountain of cushions. She sat down gingerly, but she was instantly swallowed by the cushions.

The tinkle of best china being carried on a tray alerted Tammy to Katherine entering the room, but for love or money she couldn't escape the marshmallows that were enveloping her.

Katherine openly laughed out loud as soon as she saw what had happened to Tammy. 'Oh, I'm sorry, love. I was just sorting through them, deciding which ones to take with me to mum's. It's my passion you see. I collect cushions. Well, more so cushion covers these days. I've done so since I was a child.' She set the tray down on the coffee table. 'Just throw them over the side onto the floor. This lot is going in the loft.'

'Wow. That's some collection. You are the first person I've ever met who collects cushions.'

Katherine blew out her cheeks. 'This is only a small part of it. Most of my collection is stored at mum's. Actually, I intend to have a proper sort through it whilst I'm there. I think a large donation to charity is on the cards.' Katherine lifted the teapot and began pouring into the matching teacups. 'Milk and no sugar is the way you like it, isn't it?'

'It is. Well remembered.'

'Comes with the territory. I could tell you how each of my customers takes their tea and coffee. What am I like? I should be saying *your* customers now.' She chuckled and handed Tammy a cup and saucer.

Tammy accepted it with a smile. 'I can't quite believe it yet, Katherine. Just over a week ago, I was miles away in a claustrophobic city sleeping on my friend's couch, licking my wounds, and wondering if my life would ever get any better after being dumped by my cheating boyfriend, who'd been sly enough to put the flat and business in his own name. I'd lost everything. My home. My business. My savings... But worse of all, I'd lost my self-esteem—my dignity.' Katherine gasped as she settled into her armchair with her tea. 'But then I called Uncle Ben to wish him a happy birthday, and it was as if my dearly departed parents were looking after me from heaven above, because the next thing I knew, I was on a train visiting Uncle Ben for the first time ever.' She looked into Katherine's kind eyes. 'Now here I am about to start over. Thanks to Uncle Ben and you, I have a roof over my head and I'm about to embark on a new business venture. Thank you so very much.'

Katherine's smile lit up her entire face as she shook her head. 'It should be me thanking you, Tammy my dear. You have made it possible for me to look after my mother. You were meant to come here and take over my café. It will make a much better tearoom.'

Tammy laughed with relief at hearing Katherine's acceptance of her tearoom. 'You think so?'

Katherine nodded enthusiastically. 'Yes. I wished I knew how to bake, or I would have done so myself years ago when I first bought the business. Seagull Bay is a magical place, Tammy. It makes wishes come true. It appears to know what is best for its residents before they do.' Tammy chuckled and nodded in agreement. 'And I'm not just talking about buying houses or starting businesses, either. It's been the catalyst for more blossoming relationships and marriages than I care to count.'

Tammy gasped. 'But I don't want a relationship, Katherine. I'm happy as I am on my own. Men are more trouble than they're worth.'

Katherine smiled serenely. 'If Seagull Bay intends to pair you up with your fated partner, then there's not one thing you can do about it, love.' Her eyes twinkled as she spoke. 'Now, let's get down to business and tie up these loose ends. I need to sort through the rest of my belongings and store them in the loft. The estate agent is coming to take some photos in the morning to put the house on the rental market. I need everything I don't want the renter to have access to stored away tonight. Then I intend to be on the road no later than 7 PM. I was aiming for six, but I think I was being a little too optimistic.'

Tammy listened intently to Katherine, but she didn't believe a coastal town held such mystical powers. 'Sorry Katherine. It's my fault you're behind.'

Katherine shook her head vehemently. 'Not at all. I've been sorting out as I waited for you... It's Monday when you intend to re-open isn't it?' Tammy nodded. 'Have you been able to find anyone to fill Agi's shoes?'

Tammy's brow pulled together. 'Agi?'

'Yes. Didn't I mention her to you?'

Tammy shook her head, her face crinkling, bewildered. 'No.'

'Oh dear. I've had so much *stuff* running through my head it must have slipped my mind. 'Agi used to come in part-time to help me on certain days when I was at my busiest. She would be in the kitchen cooking, and I'd make the drinks and serve. But she was offered a full-time job the day before you arrived in Seagull Bay. I thought I'd mentioned to you that I wouldn't have been able to cope without a little help from Agi.'

Tammy shook her head and then shrugged. 'No, but I'll be fine. I'm used to busy. I came from the city. The patisserie and bakery business I used to own was non-stop all day long. I'll be fine. I don't expect the same capacity here as there was in my city shop.'

Katherine furrowed her brow. 'Are you sure, Tammy? I could always ring around before I go.'

Tammy pushed the offer away with a flick of her hand. 'I'm sure. Don't worry.'

As the conversation continued, Tammy and Katherine delved into the details of the transition. They discussed backup suppliers, and local events, and combined their knowledge of the intricacies of running a successful business. Katherine's wisdom and guidance were invaluable, and Tammy felt a growing sense of confidence about her new venture.

As they finished their tea, Katherine glanced at the clock and let out a sigh. 'I should start gathering my things. It's going to be a long drive to my mother's, and I hate driving in the dark.'

Tammy stood up, eager to help. 'Let me give you a hand. It will save you some time. It's the least I can do. I'll take the boxes up to the loft for you.'

Katherine smiled appreciatively. 'Thank you, dear. That would be a tremendous help. Your young bones will do a much faster job than mine.'

They spent the next hour sorting through belongings, packing boxes, and carrying them up to the loft. With each trip, Tammy marvelled at the variety of items Katherine had accumulated over the years. From antique teacups to vintage cookbooks, there was a treasure trove of memories in those boxes.

As they finally finished, Katherine dusted off her hands and looked around the now much emptier living room. 'It's strange, isn't it? How quickly a space can transform from a home to just a house.'

Tammy nodded in agreement. 'Yes. I thought the apartment I shared with Richi was my forever home, but once my stuff was packed away before I left. I looked around and realised it was just bricks and mortar. Home is the people and memories surrounding you. But you're embarking on a new chapter Katherine, and I have a feeling spending quality time with your mum is going to make this chapter a really wonderful one.'

Katherine placed a hand on Tammy's shoulder, her eyes glistening with unshed tears. 'You've brought fresh energy to Seagull Bay, my dear. And I can't wait to see how Tammy's Tearoom flourishes under your care.'

With a final glance around, they headed for the front door. Katherine handed Tammy another set of keys. 'These are my set for the tearoom. You might need them if you decide to hire someone else to work alongside you.'

Tammy accepted the keys with a smile. 'I doubt it, but I'll hang on safely to them for you, Katherine.'

As they stood by the front door, ready to say their goodbyes, Katherine pulled Tammy into a warm embrace. 'Thank you for everything, Tammy. And remember, if you ever need advice or just a friendly chat, don't hesitate to call.'

Tammy hugged Katherine back, feeling a swell of emotion. 'You're leaving big shoes to fill, Katherine.'

Katherine chuckled. 'Well, you have big dreams to chase, my dear. I have no doubt you'll do wonders.'

Katherine picked up her handbag from the table in the hallway and they stepped outside together. Tammy stood back as Katherine locked the front door and then deposited the key in a key safe on the wall next to the door.

They headed to Katherine's car parked on the road outside her house and Katherine glanced back at the house one final time before getting into her car loaded with boxes on the back seat.

She wound down the window and smiled. 'Goodbye, my dear. I'll call you in a few days to see how you're getting on.'

Tammy nodded. 'Bye Katherine.' With one final wave, she watched her drive away, feeling a mixture of gratitude and responsibility. She was truly on her own now, with a tearoom to run and a community to serve.

As the evening sun cast a warm glow over Seagull Bay, Tammy walked away from the house Katherine used to call home, towards her new business—Tammy's Tearoom. She was excited and a little nervous about the grand opening just a couple of days away. The challenges and joys that lay ahead were uncertain, but Tammy was determined to embrace them all.

When she reached her tearoom, she noticed a figure standing in front of it, looking out at the tranquil sea. It was Declan. Tammy's heart skipped a beat at the sight of him, and a warm smile tugged at her lips.

'Hey, she called out as she approached him.

Declan turned to her, his blue eyes lighting up. 'Hey yourself. I was just enjoying the sunset.'

'It's breathtakingly beautiful, isn't it?' Tammy agreed.

'Yes, it is.'

Tammy glanced at Declan and he wasn't looking at the sunset anymore. He was studying her profile. She was thankful for the orange glow on her face hiding her burning cheeks.

They stood side by side, gazing out at the calm waters. The waves gently lapped at the shore, creating a soothing rhythm.

Tammy felt a sense of peace, a connection not just to the beauty of Seagull Bay but also to the possibilities that lay ahead.

'You know,' Declan began, his voice soft, 'I've been thinking about something.'

Tammy turned to him, intrigued. 'What is it?'

Declan's gaze met hers, his eyes earnest. 'I know Pharis and I had our friendly banter, and we've been vying for your attention in our own ways, but I want you to know that I'm here not just because of some competition. I'm here because I genuinely enjoy your company, Tammy. I think you're amazing, and I'd love the chance to get to know you better.'

Tammy felt her cheeks warm again as his words sank in. She appreciated his sincerity and the vulnerability he was showing. 'Declan, I've enjoyed spending time with you, too. And I'm open to getting to know you better as well—but just as friends.' She wasn't ready for a relationship with anyone. No matter how attractive Declan or Pharis were.

The genuine smile that was spread across Declan's face instantly vanished. 'That's fine... As friends.'

Feeling an awkward tension suddenly fall upon them, Tammy lifted her hand in a farewell gesture. 'Well, have a good evening. I need to get back. I haven't seen Uncle Ben all day.'

'You too.' Declan turned his back on her and headed for the door at the side of the tearoom. Tammy's tummy tightened as she watched him before turning around and continuing home.

Chapter ten

Banging downstairs woke Tammy. She groaned and reached for her phone to check the time. It was mid-morning. Tammy shot up into a sitting position, momentarily disorientated. What day was it? Was it her opening day?

Her eyes scanned her phone for the date. She let out a long sigh of relief and fell back into the warmth she'd just left. It was Sunday. It was the one day her uncle didn't work. The banging continued.

'What *is* he doing?'

Throwing back the cover, Tammy plunged her feet into her strategically placed slippers and reached for her dressing gown. When the cord was tied in place around her waist, she headed downstairs.

The source of the banging became clear as Tammy descended the stairs. Uncle Ben was in the kitchen, surrounded by an assortment of old photo albums, cards, and memorabilia. He looked up as Tammy entered, his face lighting up with a mix of excitement and nostalgia.

'Morning, lass,' he greeted with a grin. 'You're just in time.'

Tammy rubbed her eyes, still trying to fully wake up. 'In time for what, Uncle Ben?'

Her Uncle Ben held up a weathered envelope, his fingers carefully handling it. 'I was looking for those birthday cards you've been sending me all these years. I thought I'd have a look at them today because I need to add my recent card from you to the others.'

Tammy's grogginess quickly faded as the significance of the moment hit her. She stepped closer, a mix of curiosity and emotion welling up inside her. 'You kept them?'

Uncle Ben chuckled, nodding. 'Aye, indeed I did. Every one of them. And while I was at it, I stumbled upon some old photo albums. Haven't looked at these in years.'

Tammy's heart fluttered as she saw the albums spread out on the kitchen table. 'Wow. Are there any photos of you when you were my age, Uncle? I bet you were a head-turner when you were young.'

'Oi! I'm still a head-turner now you cheeky beggar. I'll have you know; I have many requests from my customers, asking me to pop around and sample the fish they've purchased from me.'

Tammy giggled as she poured herself a mug of tea from the teapot her uncle was keeping warm with a knitted tea cosy. 'I don't doubt that you do Uncle Ben. I bet you have to fight them off with a stick.' Ben laughed. 'In fact, I saw them all crowding you the other day. You were smiling and laughing—quite in your element you were.' Ben chuckled.

She joined Ben at the kitchen table, the anticipation building as she watched him open one of the cards she'd sent him years earlier. The picture on the front was vaguely familiar. He turned it around to show her the message she'd written inside.

Dear Uncle Ben,

Wishing you the happiest birthday ever. I hope you have glasses on so that you can read this message.

Love Tammy.

Tammy burst out laughing. 'Why on Earth did I write that?'

Ben's smile reached from ear to ear. 'Maybe because you knew I was old. Anyway, it made my day. It kept a smile on my face for weeks every time I thought of it.'

'Awww. I'm glad. I really looked forward to your cards as well, Uncle Ben. I'm ashamed to admit it to you now, but I especially loved the ten-pound notes you sent me. It was as if I knew someone out there cared for me.'

Ben reached for her hand and squeezed it. 'Of course I cared about you, lass. I just wished I'd been in circumstances that would have allowed me to raise a nipper.'

'It just wasn't meant to be uncle, but at least we are together now.'

Tammy could see her uncle's bottom lip quivering. It was clear to see he was overwhelmed with emotion. 'Yes, lass.'

He quickly turned away and reached for a tattered brown album. When he opened it, a faint smell of mustiness filled the air.

Tammy smiled at the old grey photos of fishing boats, which changed to coloured photos as he turned the pages. She wasn't at all surprised. 'Oh wow. Are those boats you used to fish in, Uncle Ben?'

'Aye lass. I took a snapshot of every single one of them.' As he turned the pages, the photos of boats stopped and were replaced with snapshots of people. Ben stopped at a photo of a young girl.

'Well, I never.'

'What? Who is it uncle?'

'It's-it's Nicola—your mum.' Tammy gasped as she stared at the features of a child who resembled her when she was just a few years older than the girl in the image. 'I must have taken them when she lived with me for a while.

Her uncle continued to turn the pages, and the old photos lost their white border as they became visibly more up-to-date. There was a young couple smiling with a baby and then as he went on, the couple appeared with a toddler in the place of the baby. Candid moments captured of the small family filled the pages.

Tammy's emotions swirled like a stormy sea. She saw images of family outings, birthday celebrations, and everyday moments. The unmistakable smiling faces of her parents beaming with love, their joy evident in every photograph.

Uncle Ben pointed to a picture of her parents holding her as a baby. 'Look at that, lass. Your mum and dad were so proud and happy. You were the centre of their world.'

Tammy's throat tightened and she blinked back tears. 'I can't believe you found these, Uncle Ben. It's the best day of my life... I-I wished I'd known them.'

Uncle Ben's hand found hers on the table, giving it another reassuring squeeze. 'I know, lass. They were wonderful people, but they did leave you with a gift—their love and these memories.'

Touched by his words, Tammy smiled through her tears. 'Thank you, Uncle Ben. That means a lot to me.'

He patted her hand gently. 'It was about time I took a trip down memory lane and I'm so glad I did, otherwise, I might not have come across these for years... And speaking of memories, I recognise this envelope here.' He reached for an envelope tucked within the pages of a book and handed it to Tammy.

Curious, Tammy opened it carefully. Inside were a series of old polaroids of her parents when they were young, in love, and starting their life together. She gasped as she saw her mother in her wedding dress, her father looking dashing in his suit, a sour-faced couple on one side with a much younger Ben, and a smiling younger couple on the other side. She rubbed her thumb tenderly over the images of her parents, feeling like she had unearthed hidden treasures.

'These were taken by a friend of your parents on their wedding day,' Uncle Ben explained. 'They gave me these photos for safekeeping, and I completely forgot about them.'

Tammy's eyes shimmered with tears as she looked at the photographs. 'I can't believe these exist.' She pointed to the sour-faced older couple. 'Who are they?'

Her uncle huffed. 'Believe it or not, that's my sister and her husband... Your grandparents.'

Tammy gasped. These were the grandparents who wanted nothing to do with her when her parents passed away. 'And the couple standing next to my father?'

Ben squinted as he looked at the photo. 'I recognise them, but I don't have a name right now. I'll think about it. There were a lot of friends at their wedding—not much family—but lots of friends.'

'Thank you, Uncle Ben.'

He winked at her. 'Well, it's not every day you turn another year older and get to surprise yourself with your own treasures.'

She spent the next hour with her Uncle Ben reminiscing about the times in the photographs. Tammy wanted to know in detail about her parent's wedding and her own Christening, telling her uncle she'd been to Reverend Townsend's church and after speaking to him he'd fetched the wedding and Christening ledger for her to look at. Ben shared stories about her parents and their adventures. Tammy's heart felt lighter as the memories connected her to the past, grounding her in the love that had shaped her.

Tammy spread out the photos of the wedding and her christening on the table, the memories of the ancient wedding and baptising ledgers still fresh in her mind. Now she was eager to soak up everything Ben could recall about those long-ago events.

'When I saw my parents' signatures in the wedding ledger, I tried to imagine what the ceremony had been like. What my parents were wearing. Whether my mother had a bouquet. Can you tell me a bit more about it after seeing these photos Uncle Ben?' Tammy urged; her eyes bright. 'Reverend Townsend said their wedding ceremony was one of the first he performed.'

Ben chuckled and leaned back in his chair, a reminiscent smile on his face as he stared at the photo of her radiant mother in a flowy white dress on her father's arm. 'Oh it was a grand affair and a beautiful sunny day, much like today. The whole town turned out and some of the older women had been at the church since dawn decorating it with wildflowers. Goodness me, it was beautiful. They knew your parents were getting married on a shoestring and wanted it to be really special for them. Heck, your mother even made her own dress, spending months hand-stitching lace to add to the dress she'd bought.'

Tammy gazed at the photo, tracing the intricate bodice. She could almost see her mother bent industriously over the fabric, needle and thread stitching lovingly.

'Your father Chris was so nervous that morning,' Ben continued with a faraway smile. 'He was convinced your mother had made a mistake agreeing to marry someone from outside Seagull Bay when she could have had her pick of any man in the town.'

'He looked so distinguished in his suit,' Tammy mused, picking up the photo of her father's tearful grin as he watched Nicola walk down the aisle.

'Distinguished? The man was so pale his freckles stood out like spilled gingerbread crumbs!' Ben said with a hearty laugh at his own joke. 'I remember he was so nervous he was trembling at the altar. But from the moment he turned around at the first notes from the church organ and saw your mother walk down the aisle, if the church would have collapsed around him I don't think he'd have noticed.'

Tammy stared at the photo as Ben recalled the special moment and pictured it happening in her mind as he spoke, imagining the joyful celebration and her parents gazing lovingly into each other's eyes in the centre of it all.

'Now the boisterous reception—all I can tell you about that is the music was loud, and the dancing spilled from the church hall into the streets. Those were the days when I liked more than one pint of beer,' he chuckled.

Shuffling through more photos, Tammy came across one of herself as a baby, her little baptised feet peeking from beneath a lace gown. That prompted her to ask about her own christening.

'Reverend Townsend mentioned Mother wanted him to do something unique for the record book that day,' she prompted, recollecting what the reverend had told her about that day.

'Ah yes!' Ben exclaimed. 'Always the creative soul, your mother. She pulled out a small pot of special non-toxic ink and asked the reverend if she could dip your feet in it and press your tiny feet into the baptismal ledger along with your name and birth date. Thought it would be a lasting memento of the occasion.'

Tammy smiled, remembering the tiny footprints she had seen beside her own name. 'How did Reverend Townsend feel about that?'

'Oh, he was quite flabbergasted at first,' Ben said. 'I dare say no one had ever asked such a thing before in all his years. But after considering it, I believe he was rather touched by the notion.'

Ben went on to describe the event fondly, recalling Reverend Townsend's deep voice booming through the chapel, her mother crying tears of joy as Tammy was sprinkled with holy water, and her father handing out cigars to the guests afterward because this was in a time before the smoking ban was introduced.

'You hardly fussed at all through the whole affair, just gazing around with wide eyes at all the faces beaming down at you,' said Ben.

Tammy could almost see her baby self being cradled lovingly in her mother's arms, the smiling guests, the proud tears in her father's eyes. It all seemed more real now, not just a story but a true moment experienced with people who had loved her deeply.

As Ben continued reminiscing, she hung on every detail. The way her father had insisted on taking a family portrait with his new camera after the ceremony, her mother's radiant smile as she held Tammy at the reception and greeted well-wishers, how the heavenly scent from the lilac sprigs woven into her hair had lingered for days, prompting whoever saw her after the ceremony to smell her hair.

Tammy realised she didn't need memories first-hand to still feel connected to the past. Her uncle's stories painted the events in vivid colour until she could nearly step into the scenes herself. She found herself brushing tears away as Ben described her parents slow dancing at the reception, her father whispering sweet nothings into her mother's ear.

By the time Ben's recollections came to a natural close, Tammy's heart felt so full it might burst. She now understood her parents not just as names in an old ledger or faces in faded photographs, but as real people whose love still lingered, waiting to be found again.

'Thank you,' she whispered, her voice heavy with emotion. 'For bringing them back to life for me.'

Ben patted her hand tenderly. 'They were the best people I've ever known. They'd have been so proud of you, my dear.'

Tammy hugged him tightly, knowing she couldn't have asked for a better living link to the past. The sun's rays cast a golden glow over the cosy kitchen. Tammy knew this day would stay etched in her heart forever.

She picked up two photos. One of the wedding day and one of the Christening. 'Do you mind if I hang onto these for my opening day Uncle Ben? It will make it all the more special.'

'All these photographs are yours now, Tammy. I want you to have them all.'

Tears brimmed on her lower lashes, threatening to spill. 'Oh, Uncle Ben...are you sure?'

'Of course I'm sure. I was meant to find them to give to you. It was probably Nicola and Chris who prompted me.'

Tammy flung her arms around her uncle. 'Thank you-thank you-thank-you.'

'It's my pleasure. Now get yourself ready and down to that tearoom of yours. I'll gather the photos together and put them in your room while you're there.

'Thanks Uncle Ben.' Tammy kissed his cheek and then glided upstairs to get ready, feeling as if she was floating on air. She couldn't wait to get to the tearoom to make the last-minute preparations for tomorrow's grand opening.

Chapter eleven

Tammy practically skipped down the seaside lane, humming happily to herself and unable to contain her excitement. Today was dedicated to putting the finishing touches into her new tearoom before the grand opening tomorrow. She had so many little tasks left to complete—adjusting pictures, stocking display jars, testing recipes. There was still much to do, but she buzzed with eager energy, ready to check items off her list.

With a bubbling excitement in her chest, Tammy approached the charming tearoom, her eyes taking in every inch of it. The soft morning sunlight cast a warm glow on the exterior, making it feel even more inviting. Her eyes lifted to the new freshly painted sign above the door and her heart swelled. Thanks to Reverend Townsend putting the word out and Pharis agreeing to help, everyone would know the café was now a tearoom. Not only that, they'd know she was now the new proprietor too.

Hurrying over to the blue door, she pushed her key into the lock. She had a long list of last-minute details to attend to, but every task was going to be a labour of love.

Stepping inside, Tammy breathed deeply. The freshly painted lemon walls and ocean-themed decor filling the cosy space never failed to lift her spirits. This charming tearoom represented her dreams coming true, a chance to start fresh in idyllic Seagull Bay.

Tammy rolled up her sleeves and got to work. She spent the next hour tweaking the decor, fussing about, adjusting the quaint pictures on the walls, arranging the tables and chairs just so, and ensuring that every decorative element contributed to the cosy atmosphere she wanted to create, stepping back periodically to judge the overall look.

The dangling shells of the wind chimes tinkled as she moved them near the front window where they could best catch the ocean breeze. The charming carved whale figurines were carefully rearranged into a playful pod on the round oak hostess stand, and the large seascape painting of a lighthouse was centred precisely next to the cork noticeboard. Her heart swelled with a mix of anticipation and nerves—her dream was about to become a reality.

Satisfied with the decor, Tammy headed to the kitchen to take stock of supplies. She had already bought all the necessary ingredients but wanted to organise the large stainless steel commercial refrigerator. Soon jars of clotted cream, lemon curd, fruit jams, and delicate finger sandwiches filled the shelves. The personalised chrome Earl Grey and breakfast tea canisters were given prime real estate on the wooden countertop next to the complicated coffee-making machine.

Tammy was just giving the gleaming oval hostess stand one final polish when the jingle of the doorbell announced a new presence. Tammy turned to see Pharis' grinning face as he strolled into the tearoom with a huge wicker picnic basket in hand and a mischievous grin playing on his lips.

'Pharis! What are you doing here?' Tammy exclaimed, momentarily distracted from her flurry of activities.

'Afternoon, busy bee,' he replied cheerfully. 'Thought you could use a quick break from all this hard work before your big day. How about we take a little break and have a picnic on the beach?" He held up the overflowing basket as temptation, the delicious scents of fresh bread and salmon wafting from it.

Tammy's eyes widened in surprise, and she glanced around at the still-incomplete tearoom. 'Oh Pharis, that's so thoughtful and I appreciate the gesture, but there's so much left to do...' Tammy gestured helplessly at the room behind her.

He waved a dismissive hand. 'Trust me, Tammy. The tearoom will still be here after you've eaten lunch. You need a moment to relax.' Tammy opened her mouth to protest. 'It'll keep for an hour,' Pharis cajoled, his hazel eyes twinkling. 'You need to refuel or you'll run out of energy. Come on, I've brought some food samples for you to try of my farm-fresh food too, thought they might be nice additions to your menu.'

As much as Tammy wanted to protest, she couldn't deny that the idea of a brief escape was appealing. Pharis made a convincing case—a short break would renew her focus. And those samples could be perfect for the tearoom if they were as tasty as the other ingredients he'd provided. 'Alright, you've convinced me, but only for a little while. I can't afford to be away for too long,' she conceded, grabbing a blanket for them to sit on. 'I can spare no more than forty-five minutes for this picnic lunch.'

Pharis grinned triumphantly. 'Deal.'

They found a quiet cosy spot on the beach away from the holidaymakers and Tammy spread out the chequered blanket she'd brought with her. Soon they were settled on it with a light breeze ruffling their hair.

Pharis unpacked an amazing spread—freshly baked bread still warm from the oven, goat cheese and fig preserves, smoked salmon and dill sandwiches, mini quiches, and dainty pastries that looked almost too beautiful to eat. For dessert, tiny lemon tarts that made Tammy's mouth water just looking at them. Tammy couldn't help but smile at the effort he'd gone to.

As they savoured the flavours, Pharis shared stories about the origins of the different foods and their potential appeal to her customers. He had such passion when discussing his ideas for new programs and partnerships he was considering with his own business. His easy-going charm and entrepreneurial spirit captivated Tammy, and the food samples he'd brought were absolutely delicious—she told him they'd be perfect additions to her menu. Tammy found herself getting lost in his enthusiasm, gradually forgetting about the mounting to-do list waiting for her back at the tearoom.

Time seemed to stretch and slow down, and Tammy's initial worries melted away. She felt surprisingly at ease with Pharis, his carefree attitude infectious. For the first time in a while, she was able to let go of the stress that had been building up within her.

Glancing at her watch, Tammy saw almost an hour had passed. 'Oh dear, I really should be getting back,' she said, scrambling up and brushing crumbs from her dress.

Just then, not far from them, she noticed a lone figure strolling along the shoreline, accompanied by a massive dog. Her heart skipped a beat, and a twinge of awkwardness settled in her chest. She recognised Declan's familiar gait. Tammy felt suddenly self-conscious about being discovered picnicking with Pharis.

'Erm, Pharis,' Tammy began, her voice tinged with uncertainty, 'I think we have company.'

Pharis turned to follow her gaze, and a knowing grin spread across his face. 'Looks like your friend Declan is taking a stroll.'

As Declan approached, his dog playfully bounding alongside him, Tammy felt a sudden surge of guilt. She forced a smile and gave a hesitant wave. 'Good afternoon, Declan.' Declan drew closer and eyed their cosy setup with thinly veiled irritation. 'Taking Fernando for a walk?' It was a stupid question as it was clearly evident he was. Tammy attempted to act casual. She wanted Declan to see there was nothing romantic happening with the beach picnic.

However, the usually friendly Declan walked past without so much as a nod, a hint of annoyance marring his handsome features. Tammy's heart sank, and she couldn't shake the feeling that their once-solid friendship had been strained by something more than his display of grumpiness.

Once Declan was out of earshot, Tammy couldn't help but feel a sense of frustration building within her. Tammy turned her gaze back to Pharis, embarrassment turning to indignation. 'Well! That was rather rude, wasn't it?'

Pharis merely chuckled. 'Don't let it trouble you. Some folks just have no manners.' His nonchalant reply only irked Tammy more, but she bit her tongue.

Irritation about the whole awkward situation as well as feeling guilty about the time she'd wasted bubbled to the surface. 'Pharis, thanks for the picnic. It was a lovely gesture, but I really should get back. I can't afford to waste any more time.'

Pharis raised an eyebrow, his playful demeanour not diminishing. 'I was only trying to get you to relax for a spell,' holding up his hands innocently. 'I told you we'd only be here for an hour. We've got a few minutes left.'

Tammy huffed, her irritation directed at both the situation and Pharis. 'What?! I haven't got minutes to waste. Y-you show up unannounced, delaying me with this picnic when there is still so much to do for the opening. I need to be back in the tearoom making final preparations. This was nice, but I have work to do.'

Pharis leaned back, his amusement evident. 'Alright, alright. No need to get all riled up. Let's pack up then.'

Tammy hurriedly began packing up the remains of their lunch, movements sharp with frustration. As her irritation began to ebb, a twinge of guilt replaced it. She realised that her outburst had been directed at the wrong person. Pharis had only been trying to offer a moment of respite. 'Look...I appreciate the thought,' Tammy replied, softening slightly. 'But I really must get back. Enjoy the rest of your afternoon!'

As they parted ways and Tammy stormed off the beach, her frustration dissipated into the salty breeze. Perhaps she had overreacted, but Declan's cold shoulder had hurt. She thought they were becoming friends. With a sigh, she resolved to clear the air with him soon. She knew she had to make things right with Pharis as well. She wasn't looking forward to being in both of their company tomorrow, and the feelings of awkwardness their meeting would bring.

Taking a deep breath, she headed back to the tearoom with a renewed determination to mend her relationships and ensure that her grand opening day went off without a hitch. For now, she had work to do—with the afternoon half gone, there was no time for distractions if she wanted to be ready for tomorrow's big reveal.

The next several hours flew by in a flurry of activity. Display jars were filled with whimsical cookie assortments. Sea turtle sugar cookies, octopus ginger snaps, and more. The chalkboard menu items were carefully written in Tammy's best cursive script, and test batches of scones and miniature fruit tarts were baked to perfection.

By the time Tammy placed a 'Reserved' sign on a quaint table set for two by the front window for her uncle tomorrow, the summer sun was setting. She stood back and let out a long breath, gazing around her dream tearoom. It was really finished. Everything shined, sparkled, and dazzled—a charming seaside retreat.

Weary but thoroughly satisfied, Tammy locked up and wandered down to the beach as the setting sun cast rippling pink and orange light across the water's surface. She sank into the soft sand, listening to the rhythm of the waves, letting them calm her whirring mind.

Despite the day's stresses, she was filled with eager anticipation for tomorrow's opening. This charming tearoom represented a fresh start, and soon locals and tourists alike would be enjoying this special spot. She said a silent prayer of thanks for the twist of fate that had brought her here.

As dusk faded to twilight, Tammy lingered until the first stars dotted the violet sky. Ambling back home, she passed by the darkened windows of the pub and caught a glimpse of Declan sitting at the bar talking to Oliver. Though still stung by his morning brush-off and his odd hostility, she resolved to be the bigger person and clear the air tomorrow. This was her new beginning—her fresh start—and she refused to let anything dampen her optimism.

Back at her cosy cottage—her new shared home with her beloved uncle, Tammy enjoyed a late supper with him, recounting the day's accomplishments. Once in bed and snuggled under the quilt, her eyelids dropping, she imagined her customers' happy chatter and the tinkling of teacups filling her tearoom. Letting the soothing vision carry her to sleep, she dozed off with a blissful smile, ready to embark on this bright new adventure.

Chapter twelve

The next morning, as the sun peeked over the horizon, Tammy stood in front of her tearoom, a sense of excitement and anticipation bubbling within her. After spending the previous day finalising all the little details, making sure everything was perfect for the grand opening, she was finally ready.

The sandwich board was in position outside the shop and the dozen multi-coloured balloons she'd had blown up at the card shop were bobbing about above it, dancing to the invisible music of the soft warm sea breeze. Tammy looked up at the freshly painted sign hung in its rightful place above the window, bearing the words 'Tammy's Tearoom' in elegant letters, a tribute to her journey and the love she had poured into this new venture. All she needed now was for the tables, chairs, and parasols stored behind the tearoom to be brought out, but Katherine had told her a local gentleman went around each morning doing such jobs for all the local tradespeople, Tammy had been in grateful awe when she'd told her.

Uncle Ben came over from his fish cart to join her outside, his smile warm and proud. 'Ready for the big day, lass?'

Tammy turned to look at him, returning the smile, and nodded, her heart fluttering with a mix of nerves and exhilaration. 'I think so, Uncle. It's a new beginning, just like the sunrise over the sea.'

He chuckled and patted her back. 'You've got this, Tammy. You're carrying the legacy of your parents and your own determination. I have no doubt it will be a success. I'll pop in a little while when I see it's not too busy.'

'I have a special table all ready for you, Uncle.'

'Bless you.'

The postman she served a couple of days ago walked past whistling merrily, pulling the red postal cart behind. He stopped and dipped his head in with a greeting. 'Morning Ben. Morning Tammy.' They chorused good morning simultaneously. 'I've put the word out Tammy about you taking over the café, turning it into a tearoom, and I was sure to remind whoever I came into contact with that you are still continuing with the breakfast menu, but there would be other food served too. I think the response was quite positive overall.'

Tammy's tummy pinched. Did that mean there was some negative feedback?

'Thank you. That's very kind.'

He continued walking as he spoke. 'It's my pleasure. The sandwich you made for me was lovely. I'll call in for another one later on.'

'Wonderful. I look forward to seeing you again.'

Tammy turned to her uncle and made an excited face. 'I'll see you shortly.' She kissed his cheek and walked in, surveying the tearoom with a smile before tying her hair back and slipping into her apron.

She busied herself brewing coffee and turning on the large griddle and cooker ready to begin cooking; she wanted at least some of the breakfast food cooked and ready to go before her first customers arrived.

Forty minutes later, the morning breakfast foods were in hotpots, keeping warm for the first few customers. Tammy made her way to the entrance door and turned around to survey her new domain, seeing what her first customers would see.

The intimate tables were set with fresh flowers and soft music played from hidden speakers, filling the room with a soothing melody, and the cakes and pastries she'd spent a day baking were proudly displayed in the cooler glass cabinet. Everything sparkled and shone. She was ready. All she needed now were customers.

The tinkle of the bell above the door behind her set her pulse racing. She set a smile on her face and turned to greet her first customer. A woman with immaculate hair, whom Tammy guessed to be in her fifties smiled brightly at her.

'Good morning Tammy my dear, and welcome to Seagull Bay. Katherine asked me to call in and show you a friendly face.' She extended her hand. 'I'm Christine. I own the local hair salon.'

Tammy shook Christine's hand. 'Awww. How lovely of her. Hello Christine and thank you. I'm a bag of nerves and your wonderful smile is just what the doctor ordered. Can I get you anything? As you are my first ever customer, it's on the house.'

Christine shook her head. 'Oh bless you, but I'll be paying my way. I want this venture to be successful for you. Can I have a flat white expresso coffee and a toasted teacake to go, please? I have an early client and I'm not fully awake yet.' She laughed at herself.

'Thank you.' Tammy stepped behind the counter and set about making the coffee first. 'Do you take sugar, Christine?'

'No thank you. I'm sweet enough.' She giggled again. Tammy smiled to herself as she spooned in espresso granules. 'The place looks amazing, by the way. You've added your own charm.'

'Thank you. I wanted to add a touch more of the coastal town feel. You don't think I've gone overboard with the wooden whale figurines, do you?'

'Not at all. They are my favourite part of the décor revamp.' Tammy sighed with relief. 'I notice you've kept the cork noticeboard. That's good because I wanted to ask you if I could pin up a small A5 sized poster.'

'Of course. Pin away. I'm just nipping in the back kitchen to make your teacake.'

While Tammy was toasting the teacake, the doorbell jingled, alerting her of a new customer. Tammy's tummy turned over with excitement. She heard Christine welcome them and begin chatting. Tammy was slightly relieved. She didn't want to risk going out and burning Christine's order. Then the jingle of the doorbell sounded again.

Tammy grimaced as she began buttering the teacake. *Another customer already?* 'Be with you shortly!' At the bakery she'd shared with Richi, he'd been the face to greet people, taking orders and money, and then making drinks and serving food from the cabinets out front. Tammy had stayed in the back, doing all the behind-the-scenes work needed for their bakery.

She quickly bagged the teacake and took it out into the tearoom for Christine, who was now standing by the counter again. There was a face she didn't recognise who, by his attire, was someone on vacation. The other person was Pippa.

'Good morning,' she beamed at both the new customers as she placed Christine's order down in front of her.

The holidaymaker smiled.

'Happy grand opening day,' said Pippa, making jazz hands.

Tammy chuckled. 'Thank you.'

Christine held her purse open, ready to delve into it. 'How much do I owe you, Tammy? And before you protest again. I'm paying.'

Tammy grinned and turned to the till to ring up her order. Thankfully, it was very similar to the one they'd used in her previous bakery shop. 'Four pounds fifty please, Christine.'

Christine handed her the correct change. 'Thank you, and I'll try and pop in later. But it all depends on how busy I'm going to be. The new pet grooming part of my shop is also having its grand opening today, so I'm hoping the pets will bring their owners for a trim as well.' Christine laughed all the way to the door. 'Cheerio.'

Pippa shook her head with a smile. 'I love that woman. She hasn't changed one bit since I was little.' Pippa pointed to the chalked menu on the wall behind the counter. 'Two bacon and egg butties on white bread to go please with runny eggs and tomato ketchup on just one of them. Oh, and can you butter the bread of the one without ketchup?'

'I'll have exactly the same, please,' said the holiday maker with a grin.

Tammy nodded and smiled, listening keenly and trying not to show her rising panic as she heard the tinkle of the door again. 'Sure thing, coming right up.' She darted into the kitchen to quickly make the orders, hoping they wouldn't ask for drinks too. She wasn't sure she could manage numerous different orders.

Pippa oohed and ahhed at the cakes on display. 'You know what? I think I'll take two slices of lemon cake and two slices of coffee and walnut cake too, Tammy. My dad and aunt will love a piece of homemade cake with their cups of tea.'

Tammy called back. 'Okey-dokey.' I'll bag them shortly. Right about now, she wished she was an octopus. What was it she'd said to Katherine about managing on her own?

As the first customers started to trickle in, Tammy greeted them with a genuine smile and a warm welcome. The scent of freshly brewed coffee and baked pastries filled the air, creating an inviting atmosphere that drew people in. Come mid-morning, the tearoom buzzed with laughter, chatter, and the clinking of cups.

Ben came in and greeted the locals he knew, immediately falling into the role of host, chatting with the customers, making them feel at home, and ensuring that everyone was having a wonderful time. Tammy watched him with pride, grateful for his unwavering support. But just before lunchtime, he approached the counter with a grimace. 'Sorry lass. I have to get back to the cart. Ned who's watching it for me wants to come in here for his lunch.'

Tammy reached over the counter grabbed hold of his arm and squeezed it warmly. 'Thanks Uncle Ben, I don't know what I would have done without you. I'll see you back home later on.'

'Okay Lass. Don't work too hard, you hear? Or else you'll be plum worn out for tomorrow.'

Tammy chuckled, her chest glowing with love for her uncle. 'I won't.'

But with her uncle's absence came a new wave of customers. Tammy pressed a smile onto her face, but behind it, she was screaming. She was totally overwhelmed. The orders were backing up and customers who had yet to be served stood at the back of the room, watching her every move. She tried her best to make drinks while things were cooking in the kitchen beyond the main tearoom, but she was sure she could smell burning—and she definitely heard someone moaning. Her stomach pulled into a tight knot.

The tinkling of the bell sounded out again and she had to stop herself from audibly groaning. She loved how busy she was, but she also hated how slow she was and grimaced at the thought she might be letting Katherine's previous customers down.

Katherine was right. This gig was a two-person job.

Forcing a smile on her face, she pushed the plastic lids on the latest order of teas to go and turned around to face her next customer. The smile slid from her face when she saw Declan.

'I-I want to apologise for ignoring you when you greeted me on the beach yesterday.' The knot pulled tighter in her tummy and her heart sped up. Tammy glanced past Declan to the curious faces who had heard what he'd said and were taking mini steps forward to get a better earshot of the conversation Declan was trying to orchestrate.

Tammy shook her head, dismissing his apology. The reality was, she *really* wanted to know why he had been so rude. She wanted to know if it had been anything to do with her being with Pharis. Whether he was curious as to whether their picnic was an innocent one, or one that had intimate connotations.

'No-no. It's fine—really.'

'But it's not fine...I acted appallingly.' A few women giggled and whispered to each other. Tammy could feel her cheeks heating.

She held her hands up to stop him. 'NO! Really, Declan. It's fine.'

His eyes opened wide, and his brow shot up as he leaned backward from her mini outburst. Tammy thought his reaction was a bit over-exaggerated. She hadn't raised her voice *that* loudly. Declan suddenly began sniffing the air. 'Is-is that burning I can smell?'

Tammy's hand shot to her mouth. 'Oh no! The sausages!'

Declan slipped behind the counter and shot past her. 'Don't worry. I got this. You continue serving and making the drinks. I'll see to the hot food.'

She was flabbergasted. This was her business. She didn't want to share a kitchen with *another man*. She'd been there, done that, and had the t-shirt stolen from her back by the very man she'd shared the experience with. Opening her mouth to protest, Tammy quickly shut it, when a family of four squeezed into the tearoom behind the already long queue.

She smiled at the gossiping women and turned her back on them to complete the hot drinks order. A few minutes later, Declan appeared with four bags, placing them down on the counter before disappearing back through the door again. Tammy's mouth dropped open. He'd found the stickers to mark what the contents were, and each paper bag was marked up appropriately.

Tammy looked over at the four customers who'd been waiting for them. 'Orders 27, 28, 29 and 30?' They stepped forward and claimed the bags and appropriate drinks. Two said their thanks and left. The other two asked for cupcakes. Tammy bagged up the cakes and took their payments. Her stiff shoulders eased a little as she took card payments with her new card machine. This was easier, not having to worry about the food cooking side of things out back.

'Thank you for your custom. Please call again,' she smiled sweetly. The next customers stepped forward. Her smile brightened. 'Good afternoon. What can I get you?'

As the day steadily came to a close, Tammy stood at the door to the kitchen and peered in. Declan had cleaned the kitchen, and it was as spotless as when she'd opened up that morning. 'You didn't have to do that.'

'A good chef takes pride in his workplace,' was all he replied. There was still an air of awkwardness between them.

'I really appreciate your help, Declan. Apparently, Katherine used to have someone help her three days a week. I think I was a little naïve. Because I had my own bakery business recently, I thought I'd be okay and be able to cope on my own.'

'Are you looking to hire someone now?'

Tammy puffed out her cheeks. 'Absolutely. Do you know anyone in this town with experience of working in catering?'

'As a matter of fact...I do, and that person only wants a few part-time days of work as well.'

'Perfect!'

'Is there any way of speaking to them this evening? I could really do with help...possibly tomorrow again.'

'Okay. Fire away What do you want to know?'

Tammy's eyebrows drew together. 'What? I'd prefer to speak to them in person if you don't mind.'

'You are. I'm the applicant.'

'You?!'

'Yes, me... Or will your *boyfriend* have something to say about it?'

'Boyfriend? I don't have a boyfriend. And even if I did, this is *my* business.'

'So you and Pharis aren't an item?'

'What? No!'

'Then what was that cosy little picnic on the beach yesterday?'

'A friend who happens to be my supplier was being considerate and killing two birds with one stone. He pulled me away from the tearoom for a break while showing me samples from his farm shop... Not that it's got anything to do with you!'

Declan's face blanched. 'Oh.'

'Yes, oh indeed.'

'I suppose I've shot myself in the foot now, haven't I?'

'YES!' Declan grabbed his belongings from off the side and walked past Tammy, heading for the door. 'No...no. Wait! I'm sorry. It's just that...I came here to Seagull Bay after a terrible break-up. My bark is worse than my bite—I promise. It's just taking a lot for me to trust men again.'

Declan turned around and walked right up to Tammy. He was so close she could smell his cologne under the smell of cooking now clinging to his clothes and hair. 'I'm sorry. If it's some consolation, that's exactly what happened to me.'

Tammy was overwhelmed with emotion. It had been a tough day. Even though she didn't want a relationship, she found she was disappointed he wasn't into girls... Yet still, she didn't want to lose Declan's friendship. Her mouth dropped open. 'Your boyfriend cheated on you, too?'

Declan frowned and scoffed as he shook his head. 'No-no. Not a boyfriend...my *girlfriend*.'

Tammy's heart soared. 'Oh...sorry. Wrong end of the stick.'

He grinned. 'Rather!' He held her gaze and she could feel her heart hammering as it picked up pace. 'So?'

'Huh?' She was being sucked into his tropical blue pools again.

'The job.'

She blinked to break the trance. 'Oh yes. Three days a week. But won't it clash with the lunchtime shifts at the pub?'

'I work all the evening shifts, and the lunchtime rota is shared out between Pippa, Pippa's Aunt Morgan, and myself, so I could work any day. Do you know which days were Katherine's busiest?'

Tammy shook her head. 'All she said was they changed depending on the time of year. I suppose I could call her and ask.'

'Okay. I'll wait until I hear from you about working tomorrow. He grabbed a pen and notepad and scribbled down his number, handing it to Tammy. 'I'll stay close tomorrow—just in case. Call me if you get busy.' He flashed her a smile that made her legs go weak, and then turned around and left.

Tammy locked the door behind him, rested her back against it, and sighed. She looked up. 'What are you doing to me Mum and Dad? What was your devious plan bringing me here?' She looked across to their wedding photograph resting against the side of the till. Her parents smiled back at her.

Act three – Chapter thirteen

The next day wasn't half as busy as the grand opening day had been, and Tammy didn't know whether to be relieved or disappointed. Yet, she still had a nice steady flow of customers that were manageable on her own and they kept her on the go all day. She even managed to come from behind the counter and spend some quality time talking to each one of her customers, getting to know more about the locals and chitchatting with the holidaymakers, finding out where they came from and how long they were staying in Seagull Bay.

The next hour continued to bring a steady stream of customers to the tearoom that kept Tammy bustling about, serving delicious treats, and engaging in pleasant conversations. With each interaction, she felt a deeper sense of connection to the locals and the visitors, appreciating the genuine conversations and warm smiles that were exchanged.

Just after the early morning rush, Tammy finally got the chance to drop Declan a quick text letting him know that she was managing well on her own for the day.

Hello Declan, I'm so sorry I haven't called you, but it turned out I've been able to cope on my own so far today. Maybe Tuesdays are going to be one of the quieter days. Anyway, am I still okay to call you tomorrow if I get busy? I know doing it this way isn't very consistent for you at the

moment but as soon as I know which are the busier days, I'll be able to offer you set working days.

Tammy

As she waited for his reply, she was elated when Reverend Townsend walked through the door.

'Good afternoon Tammy. The new sign looks fabulous.'

'Good afternoon Reverend Townsend. Thank you. I wouldn't have it if it wasn't for you—and Pharis of course,' Tammy greeted him with a cheerful smile.

'He's a good lad. He jumped at the chance when I mentioned it, even though he is super busy with the shop and the products he's creating to sell in there. His parents are really proud of him. Talking of parents, I was asked by them to invite you to the annual summer barbecue. I say annual, but this will in fact be the first one they've held in three years...or is it four?' Tammy watched amused, as the reverend grabbed his chin and gazed up at the ceiling. He shook his head. 'I digress and it doesn't matter, anyway. What does matter is that there is another one this weekend.' He fixed her with a grin, his brow lifting, causing a sea of lines on his forehead as he waited for an answer. 'Well? What answer can I pass on?'

'Oh...right.' Tammy nodded enthusiastically. 'Yes-yes. I'd love to come. I'll bake a batch of cupcakes as a thank you.'

The reverend clapped his hands together with glee. 'Wonderful. I adore your cakes.' He peered into one of the glass cabinets and pointed at one that hadn't been sliced yet. 'Is that a coffee and walnut cake I spy?'

Tammy nodded. 'It is. Would you like a slice?'

The reverend shook the palms of his hands wildly at her. 'No, not a slice. I want the entire cake.'

Tammy's eyebrows almost met her hairline. 'You want the entire cake?'

He chuckled. 'It's not just for me. I'm holding a coffee morning for the local choir. We're discussing the Christmas service today and there's nothing better to get the conversation flowing than a slice of delicious cake and a cup of tea in a bone china cup and saucer to wash it down with.'

Tammy giggled as she took the cake out from the display and carefully packed in into a cardboard cake box. 'I suppose not.' She slid the cake across the counter. 'Normally I sell the slices at £2.99 each, and there's sixteen slices there, but I'll let you have it for £35. I wouldn't have had my sign if it wasn't for your intervention.'

The reverend shook his head. 'No. I won't hear of it. I'm paying full price and that's the end of it. You've already offered free cupcakes for the barbecue.' He pulled out his wallet and handed her five crisp ten-pound notes. 'Put the change towards the ingredients for the cupcakes.' He lifted the cake and headed for the door. 'Cheerio,' he called out over his shoulder. 'I'll see you at the weekend.'

Tammy made a move to come out from behind the counter to get the door for him, but a new customer came in and held the door open.

'Goodbye, Reverend, and thanks for the custom.'

Throughout the day, Tammy also had the pleasure of meeting more of Pippa's family. Brent, Pippa's father, visited the tearoom, eager to try more of Tammy's delectable creations after being won over by the coffee and walnut cake Pippa had sampled the previous day. Their enthusiasm and genuine appreciation warmed Tammy's heart, affirming her decision to change the café into a tearoom.

As the afternoon sun began to cast a cosy glow through the tearoom's windows, Tammy took a moment to check her phone. She couldn't help but wonder if Declan was a bit miffed she hadn't needed him. Would he respond? Should she call him? It was the first time today the tearoom had been customer-free.

As if on cue, a familiar figure walked through the tearoom's door. It was Pharis. Tammy's surprise was evident in her raised eyebrows and warm smile as she greeted him. An air of awkwardness had marked their last encounter after Declan had seen them together picnicking as if they were a couple on the beach. Relations between them had definitely been strained when they'd parted company.

'Pharis, it's great to see you,' Tammy said, genuinely pleased by his visit. 'How can I help you today? Have you called in to eat?'

Pharis grinned, his eyes sparkling with mischief. He placed the hessian bag he'd brought in with him onto the counter. 'I thought I'd stop by and see how the tearoom is doing. Plus, I brought along a few more samples for you to consider. Just couldn't resist.'

Tammy chuckled, feeling a sense of ease settle between them once again. 'You're really determined to make me expand my menu, aren't you?'

'Guilty as charged,' he replied with a playful wink. 'But hey, I have a good feeling about these ones. I've added additional flavours to the chutneys.'

As they discussed the new samples, sharing insights and ideas, the atmosphere was light and friendly. Tammy felt a renewed sense of camaraderie with Pharis, grateful that their previous awkwardness seemed to have dissipated.

However, the easy atmosphere shifted when the door chimed once more, signalling the entrance of another customer. Tammy turned her attention towards the door and her heart skipped a beat as she saw Declan standing there, his piercing gaze fixed on her and Pharis.

Declan's demeanour was noticeably different—his posture more assertive, his expression determined. Without missing a beat, he strode up to the counter where Tammy and Pharis were standing.

Pharis noticed Tammy's attention had turned elsewhere and looked back at Declan.

'Hello, Tammy,' Declan greeted her, his voice carrying an undercurrent of possessiveness. 'I got your text.' He looked directly at Pharis as he made the statement with a smug smile tugging up the corners of his mouth. Then he leaned across the counter and kissed Tammy's cheek.

Tammy recoiled slightly, her surprise evident. Her hand flew up to her cheek and she fought to keep the heat rising in her from reaching her cheeks. 'Erm, Hello Declan. Then what brings you here?'

His lips quirked into a faint smile, but his eyes remained fixed on her. 'Just thought I'd check on how you're doing.'

If Tammy had fetched her best knife from the kitchen, she could have cut the palpable tension. Pharis cleared his throat and placed his hands flat on the counter, then he too leaned across, kissing Tammy on the opposite cheek. A deep rut formed in between his eyebrows as he looked from Tammy to Declan. 'I'll leave you two to catch up. I have some other business to attend to.' Tammy's jaw dropped open.

As Pharis walked away, the air seemed to grow heavy with unspoken emotions. Declan placed an elbow on the counter, leaning on it, and smiled, reminding Tammy of a cowboy in an old western movie. He lowered his voice. 'You know, Tammy, it's good to see you getting along with Pharis so well.'

Tammy's brow furrowed in confusion, her heart racing as she tried to decipher his intentions. 'What do you mean?'

His smile deepened, though it held a hint of possessiveness. 'Just making sure you're in good hands while I'm not around.'

Tammy blinked, her cheeks finally flushing with a mixture of surprise and annoyance. 'Declan, as you can see, I can handle things just fine on my own. And Pharis, *like you*, is a friend, nothing more.'

Declan's gaze held hers for a moment longer before he stepped back, a touch of amusement playing on his lips. 'Of course, Tammy. Just looking out for you...is all.'

As he turned to leave, Tammy couldn't help but feel a mixture of frustration and intrigue. The encounter had left her with a whirlwind of emotions. 'I'll eagerly await your call. Can't wait to get back in that little kitchen and show some of the locals a thing or two.'

Tammy's brows pulled together at his statement, and as the door chimed again, she couldn't shake the feeling that things were far from settled between her, Declan, and Pharis.

After the last customer left, Tammy turned the sign around to the closed sign and placed her back against the door. She allowed her head to fall back against the cool glass and let out a long ecstatic sigh.

She was exhausted, but there was still lots to do before she could leave. First, she cleaned the shop side of the tearoom, then she took a quick stock check and made a careful calculation of what had been used that day. If she could gauge stock usage and what had been sold every day, she'd be better organised next week. Lastly, she cashed up and was very pleasantly surprised with her day's efforts. Katherine had very kindly let her reset the combination to the small safe hidden away at the back of the shop. She put the day's takings inside it and thanked Katherine for being so savvy. Richi had been against her suggestion of a safe from the start. Yet another thing she'd had no say over.

With that done, she headed into the kitchen and set about baking to replenish the cakes sold. As she baked, she hummed happily to herself, and her smile never faltered. Her positive demeanour was a far cry from how it had been just a few weeks ago. Now she looked and acted like a completely different woman.

As she piped icing onto her final cake, she looked over to the refrigerator and the array of photos magnetised to it. The smiling faces of her parents seemed to confirm how she was feeling. Being here—starting the tearoom in Seagull Bay, it was meant to be.

A light rapping at the door to the shop caught her attention. Tammy quickly placed the cake in an air-tight container and popped it in the fridge. She pulled off her apron, hung it up, and hurried to the door.

A grey shaggy beard and kind old eyes were the first thing she saw through the glass door. Unlocking it, she held it open and greeted her uncle with a warm smile. 'Uncle Ben. What are you doing here? I thought you'd be in bed by now.'

'It's late, lass. I was worried. I should have known you'd still be hard at work here.' His worry lines melted away and a smile lit up his face. 'Are you finished yet?'

Tammy nodded. 'As a matter of fact, I just finished the last cake. I've cashed up and prepared for tomorrow. All I have to do now is turn the lights off and lock up.'

'Are ya hungry, lass?' Just at that moment, Tammy's tummy growled in answer. Ben looked down at it and they both chuckled. 'How's about I treat you to some fish 'n' chips at The Cheese Wedge and Pickles?'

Tammy giggled. 'Haven't you had enough of fish for the day?'

Ben winked at her. 'You can never have enough fish... Besides, they get their supplies from me, so I know it's going to be good.'

Tammy laughed as she shook her head. 'Okay, I'm sold. Let me just turn the lights off and grab my bag.'

Five minutes later, Tammy's arm was linked snuggly with her uncle's as they headed for the pub while she regaled tales of her second day in Tammy's Tearoom.

Chapter fourteen

The balloons were still floating high above the sandwich board they were tied to outside the tearoom. Tammy was amazed the local children hadn't popped them or untied them to let the helium balloons float away for their amusement.

Letting herself into the tearoom, she experienced the same excited flutter in her stomach when she switched on the lights. The smell of freshly baked cakes mixed with the fragrant flora of the flowers on the tables filling the tearoom with a welcoming and homely feeling.

Tammy put her personal items away and slipped her apron over her head, eager to start the day.

Looking out of the large shop window, she could see by the flurry of holidaymakers heading for a good place on the beach that there was a promise of good weather. That meant it would be busy.

Heading into the kitchen, she turned on the cooker and hotplate and began to prepare the food for the breakfast rush. A tinkle from the other side of the kitchen door alerted her of a customer.

'I'll be right there,' she called out, her pulse quickening.

There was another tinkle. Then another. Then another... Then another.

Customers were coming thick and fast. Tammy's heart began to gallop. She peeked out and now there was a small crowd gathering in the shop. Tammy had a sixth sense today was going to be just like it was on her opening day—non-stop-busy. Reaching her handbag, she didn't waste another second to call Declan.

He answered on the second ring.

'Declan, it's Tammy. Can you come—...'

She didn't even have to finish her sentence. 'I'm on my way.'

Less than a minute later, the tinkle of the bell above the shop door sounded out again. Tammy grimaced, then the door to the kitchen opened and Declan's blue eyes found hers as he breezed in. Her chest fluttered. 'How did you get here so quickly?'

He pointed up to the ceiling. 'The perks of living above the tearoom.'

'Ah yes. Silly me. I forgot.'

His sexy grin and twinkling eyes made her heart skip a beat. 'Want me to handle the kitchen again? Same routine?' he asked as he reached for an apron. 'Me in here and you serving customers and making drinks?'

Tammy nodded. 'I really don't mind.' She was still debating which role she preferred. Having been delegated the kitchen duties in her business with her ex, Richi. She'd thought she'd really dislike being behind the counter, but she'd loved every minute so far this week, she'd loved the customer interaction.

Declan grabbed hold of the tops of her arms to change places, spinning her around in the small kitchen, and for a brief moment, they were glued together—with him looking down at her and her looking up at him—chest to chest. Tammy's breath caught as he gazed down intently into her eyes. Still holding her arms, Declan's eyes roamed her face before resting on her parted lips.

His head slowly lowered as he if was about to kiss her and Tammy's insides went into jittery chaos. But then he hesitated, lips inches from hers. Her heart pounded wildly. Declan's smouldering eyes held a question, one she didn't know how to answer—should he continue?

As handsome as Declan was, Tammy didn't want to be kissed—she didn't know if she would ever be ready for romance again, not after how badly Richi had treated her.

'*Anyone serving*?'

Tammy turned her head and called out. 'Just coming!'

She smiled awkwardly at Declan and slipped quickly from his grasp. His intense look had left her flustered. Forcing a smile, she hurried to help the waiting customers.

The morning rush carried on with a lively momentum, and Tammy and Declan effortlessly slipped into their respective roles. Tammy's heart continued to flutter every time Declan called out from the kitchen to tell her an order was ready, and she couldn't help but notice the subtle smiles and glances he directed her way whenever they interacted throughout the morning.

The smell of freshly brewed coffee filled the air as Tammy expertly prepared cappuccinos and lattes. Her fingers danced over the complicated coffee-making machine she'd inherited from Katherine as part of the takeover, displaying a grace that came from months of practice on the coffee machine she'd once owned in her shared business with Richi.

Periodically, Declan came out from the counter to bring orders, but whenever Tammy got a chance, she would go into the kitchen and stand back watching him as he worked, showcasing his skills as he artfully arranged pastries and built sandwiches into towers of mouth-watering art, his strong hands moving with the precision and confidence that only a trained chef can muster.

Their interactions became increasingly seamless, a well-coordinated ballet of customer service and culinary prowess. When mid-morning arrived, Tammy handed an order to Declan, and their fingers brushed briefly, sending a shiver down her spine. She looked up to find Declan smiling at her, a playful twinkle in his eyes that suggested he felt the same electric spark.

Amid the rush, they found moments to exchange light-hearted banter. Tammy would make a playful comment about the weather, and Declan would respond with a witty remark that had her laughing. Their conversations flowed effortlessly, each word carrying an undercurrent of shared understanding and a growing connection.

As morning turned into midday and the pace began to ease, Tammy and Declan found themselves stealing stolen glances when they thought the other wasn't looking. When Tammy took a moment to restock the sugar packets, she felt Declan's gaze on her, and when she looked up, he quickly averted his eyes with a sheepish smile.

Lunchtime brought a short break, and they found themselves sitting at a small table near the window, sipping on cups of tea. The sunlight filtered through the gingham curtains, casting a warm glow on their faces. The conversation shifted to personal stories, childhood memories, and dreams for the future. Although Tammy omitted to go into detail about being raised in foster care, she felt a sense of comfort she hadn't experienced in a long time, a feeling that Declan was genuinely interested in getting to know her.

When she toyed with the salt cellar, Declan reached forward and caressed the tip of her missing finger. 'I spotted this last week. Is it a kitchen accident?'

Tammy had been so self-conscious about her finger all through childhood and especially in her teens, but now she barely noticed it. She shook her head. 'No, it's a result of contracting meningitis when I was a young child.' She lifted her fringe and showed him the hidden scar on her forehead. 'Thankfully, I had a skin graft done here, but it still scarred.'

'Geez, you were lucky. That's a terrible virus. I bet your parents were beside themselves with worry.'

'According to my social worker...yes they were.' Declan's brow pulled together, showing his confusion. Tammy's chest tightened. She hated disclosing her different childhood, but something about Declan's easy manner made her want to open up. 'I was raised in foster care after my parents' unexpected early deaths.'

Declan's jaw almost hit the table and his strong hand curled around hers. 'I am so sorry Tammy. I didn't mean to rake up the past.'

Tammy shook her head and smiled. 'It's fine. It was a long time ago. I don't remember them. However, coming here to Seagull Bay was possibly the best thing that ever happened to me.'

'Is that because you met me?' Declan winked cheekily.

Tammy laughed. 'Maybe that's a small part.' Declan chuckled. 'Uncle Ben found boxes of old photographs of my parents and told me so many special stories about them.'

Declan's hand found hers again. 'That's amazing Tammy. I'm so happy for you.' He scoffed and sat back in his chair. 'I wish that kind of magic could happen for me.'

Tammy's brow rose. 'How so?'

'Like you, I was raised in the system, but my parents abandoned me. I've tried to trace them over the years, but I come to a dead end every time.'

Tammy gasped. She couldn't believe how parallel their lives were. The tinkle of the bell above the door alerted them to a new customer. This time, Tammy reached across the table and grabbed Declan's hand. 'We'll find them together. I'll help you start afresh after the barbecue.'

Declan's eyes widened. 'You'd do that for me?'

'Of course. Anything for a friend.' Tammy couldn't help but notice a flicker of disappointment wash across his face. She smiled brightly at the customer as she stood up from their cosy tête-à-tête. 'Good afternoon, what can I get you?'

After the afternoon rush had dissipated, and wanting to brighten the mood between her and Declan, Tammy suggested they tackle the task of rearranging the seating area outside the tearoom. As they moved tables and chairs, their laughter filled the air, the shared effort turning into a playful competition of strength and creativity. At one point, Declan picked up a chair and pretended to carry it on his back like a weightlifter, causing Tammy to burst into giggles.

'Careful there, you might strain something,' she teased, a mischievous grin playing on her lips.

'Oh, I've been hitting the gym,' he retorted with a wink, his playful bravado earning him another round of laughter.

The chemistry between them was undeniable, a magnetic pull that drew them closer with each passing moment. Tammy's heart had transformed from a flutter to a steady rhythm, a rhythm that seemed to sync perfectly with the moments she shared with Declan, still though, she held back. Romance was not what she'd come to Seagull Bay for.

But as the late afternoon sun cast a warm, golden glow across the tearoom, Tammy and Declan found themselves standing close to each other again, it seemed that wherever he went, she was drawn to him. Their eyes locked in a shared moment of connection. The straggling customers and the surrounding tearoom seemed to fade into the background, leaving only the two of them.

Declan's voice lowered, carrying a hint of vulnerability. 'You know, Tammy, I never expected to find someone like you in Seagull Bay.'

Tammy's heart skipped a beat at his words. She had been so focused on her past and her determination to avoid romance that she had almost missed the wonderful person standing right in front of her. 'Likewise, Declan. I thought I was coming here for a fresh start, but I didn't anticipate finding a friend like you.'

Their gazes lingered, and Tammy felt a warmth spreading from her chest to every corner of her being. The connection between them was undeniable, a magnetic force that pulled them closer together.

Just as Tammy thought Declan might lean in for a kiss, a familiar tinkle of the bell above the door interrupted their moment. They both turned to see a couple entering the tearoom, hand in hand. Tammy recognised them as her new regulars who always came in late, a kind elderly couple who always shared a slice of cake.

Declan stepped back, clearing his throat, and readjusting his apron, a hint of disappointment flickering in his eyes. 'I guess we should get back to work.'

Tammy nodded, her cheeks tinged with a blush. 'Yes, we should.'

As they resumed their roles, serving the couple with smiles and small talk, Tammy couldn't help but steal glances at Declan whenever she got the chance. There was something about him—his kindness, his warmth, and the way he made her feel—that drew her in like a moth to a flame.

The day steadily came to an end, and Tammy and Declan seamlessly navigated their duties. The earlier energy in the tearoom was replaced with stillness, but underneath it, there was a subtle tension—a longing that neither of them dared to voice.

As closing time approached, Tammy couldn't shake the feeling that something had changed between them. The day had been filled with shared laughter, confidences, and lingering glances, and she couldn't deny the growing connection she felt with Declan. It was a connection she hadn't expected, one that both excited and terrified her.

Once the last customer had left, Tammy and Declan began the familiar routine of cleaning up and closing the tearoom. They moved in sync as if they had been doing this together for years. The silence between them was comfortable, a testament to the ease of their companionship.

Finally, as Tammy wiped down the last table, Declan spoke, his voice soft and filled with sincerity. 'Tammy, I know we both said we weren't looking for romance, and I meant it. But I can't deny the connection I feel with you.'

Tammy turned to face him, her heart pounding in her chest. She had been grappling with her own feelings, torn between her past and the unexpected warmth she had found in Declan's presence. 'Declan, I feel it too.'

He took a step closer, his eyes locking onto hers. 'I don't want to rush into anything, Tammy. But I also don't want to let this connection slip away.'

Tammy's hand reached out, and Declan took it in his, their fingers interlocking. 'Neither do I, Declan.'

A soft smile curved his lips, and he brought her hand to his lips, pressing a gentle kiss to her knuckles. 'Then let's take it one step at a time, okay?'

Tammy nodded, her heart filled with a mixture of hope and trepidation. 'One step at a time.'

As they locked up the tearoom together, Tammy couldn't help but feel that the balloons that had heralded the start of this day had carried with them not only the promise of good weather but also the promise of a new beginning—and as she looked into Declan's eyes, she couldn't help but wonder if they also held the promise of something more—a connection that had the potential to blossom into something beautiful.

Chapter fifteen

The next day was quiet like Tuesday had been, and Tammy was glad. She'd had a wonderful day working alongside Declan, but she needed time apart from him to assess the shift that had occurred between them.

She'd gone about her day with the same enthusiasm, but she was glad when it was time to close for the day. After going about her usual routine of cleaning, baking, cashing up, and stocktaking, Tammy realised how low on a lot of ingredients she was. She needed to get to the farm shop before it closed. After texting Mina, she absentmindedly made notes until she received the arrival alert.

Mina parked just outside the teashop in her little car and Tammy waved a friendly hello at her as she locked up the tearoom. Climbing into the car, she smiled warmly at Mina.

'Good evening, Tammy. I don't normally work in the evenings. As soon as the kids finish school, there's normally chaos in my household with homework, cooking tea, and bath time. My husband has been working from home for a few days though, so when I saw your text I thought I'd better take this fare, especially as I put my foot in my mouth and offended you last time I saw you.'

Tammy wondered how Mina was able to relay so much information without taking a breath. She shook her head. 'No, you didn't offend me and thank you for accepting my fare. I really should think about getting a car, but it's been the last thing on my mind these past couple of weeks.'

'Well, at least you know I'm just a text away,' Mina beamed.

'Exactly. It's not as if I have to drive to work anymore. A lovely stroll down the hill with a sunrise and sea view and I'm there. It's only when the stock needs replenishing that I need to use transport.'

'How is the tearoom doing? I've heard rave reviews from the locals by the way. I've been meaning to pop in and say hello but I've been flat out.'

Tammy felt warmth spread throughout her body on hearing the news. 'Oh, you don't know how relieved I am to hear that. Katherine was so well-loved by the community; I didn't know how the locals felt about me taking over. The holidaymakers appear to be happy enough with my offerings, but it's the locals' opinions that matter the most to me.'

'Well, you can put your mind at ease. Your cakes and pastries are going down a storm.' Mina glanced her way with a grin. 'There is something else that is piquing many people's interests at the moment though, Tammy. And I really shouldn't tell you, but there's a bet going around.'

Tammy frowned. 'Really? A bet? What for?'

'Who is going to win your heart?'

Tammy's eyes almost popped out. 'What? I'm not dating anyone...and I have no intention of dating anyone. I'm not interested in having a relationship. My priority is the tearoom.'

Mina nodded in agreement, her face suddenly earnest as she agreed. 'I know-I know it is. That's what I've been replying whenever people ask me what my opinion on it is.'

'Who's been asking, Mina? Why is everyone so curious about my love life?'

'Ah, you know how it is with small communities. Everyone seems to know everyone else's business. Unfortunately, because you are our newest community member, you are flavour of the month.'

Tammy sighed and crossed her arms as she looked out of the passenger door window. Ugh, well I hope I start tasting bitter soon then.' Mina laughed. Tammy's head whipped around to look at Mina's profile. 'I've just realised what you said... You said they are wondering who is going to win my heart. Are there names being thrown around, Mina?'

Mina grimaced, apprehensive about answering. 'Erm yes...two names.'

'Well? Come on, don't leave me hanging.'

Mina licked her lips obviously enjoying the build-up. 'Pharis and Declan.'

Tammy sighed. 'Well, you can tell whoever's placed a bet that it's money lost because I don't intend to date anyone.' Tammy watched Mina's shoulders drop. 'You placed a bet, didn't you?' Mina shot her a glance and grimaced again as she nodded. 'Mina!' Tammy shook her head. Suddenly curious, her eyebrows rose. 'Who did you bet on?'

Mina licked her lips again, her nerves evident. 'Pharis.'

Tammy scoffed. 'Huh. Why?'

'A little birdie told me you'd been spotted having an intimate picnic on the beach.'

Tammy threw her hands up. 'My goodness. Is nothing private in Seagull Bay?'

Mina shook her head. 'Nope.' She popped the P as she answered.

They continued in silence. Tammy got lost in her thoughts and soon Mina was winding down the country lane leading to the farm shop.

Mina parked her car in the exact same place she'd parked the first time she'd brought Tammy to the farm shop; she immediately began texting on her phone when Tammy's car door closed. Was Mina texting other locals about what she knew? Keeping them updated on the Tammy love triangle? Or was she just being paranoid? She hoped for the latter.

Tammy was a little apprehensive about seeing Pharis. Had he also heard of the rumours and bets being placed on them? Inhaling deeply for courage, she pushed open the shop door.

The same young girl as when she'd called in before was sitting behind the shop counter. She greeted Tammy with a warm smile when she saw her. 'Hello again. Have you come to replenish your stock?'

Tammy glanced around the shop quickly, looking for Pharis, but he wasn't there. There was just a middle-aged woman talking with a couple of the same age. Tammy walked towards the counter. Returning the smile. 'Hello—' she squinted her eyes as she studied the name tag, '—Ruby. Yes, I need stock for my tearoom, but I need extra this time because I promised Reverend Townsend I'd make a batch of cupcakes for the barbeque I've been invited to at the farm on Sunday.'

'Ah-ha! Are you Tammy from the tearoom? The woman my son has done nothing but talk about for the past two weeks?' said a voice from behind her. Tammy spun around to see the woman who had been talking to the couple walking towards her.

Comprehension at what she'd said suddenly made Tammy feel as if lava was bubbling underneath the surface of her cheeks. 'Erm yes, I'm Tammy.' The woman was either the mother of Declan or Pharis, but considering where she was and Pharis' Mediterranean colouring, there was a 99.9% chance the woman standing in front of her was his mum.

'I'm the one who invited you to the farm's annual barbecue...I'm Pamela, Pharis's mum.'

'Oh Pamela. It's so lovely to meet you.'

Tammy extended her hand, which Pamela took in a warm and firm handshake. 'It's a pleasure to meet you too, Tammy. My, you're just as lovely as my son described.'

Tammy couldn't help but feel a bit flustered. 'Pharis has been talking about me to you?'

Pamela chuckled, a twinkle in her eyes. 'Oh, he can't stop talking about the tearoom and how you've breathed new life into it... And, well, maybe a few other things too. Goodness, he must have spent three days solid making the sign for it.' Tammy's cheeks flushed deeper, and she nervously tucked a strand of hair behind her ear. 'I hope he's been saying good things.'

Pamela grinned. 'He has nothing but praise for your hard work, Tammy.' She then leaned in closer, her voice dropping to a conspiratorial whisper. 'Phil, my husband and I actually knew your parents—Nicola and Chris.'

Tammy's eyes widened with surprise. 'You did?'

'Yes,' Pamela replied, her gaze drifting to a distant memory. 'Your parents first saw each other in The Cheese Wedge and

Pickles, but they got to know each other better here on the farm. Your father was a handsome young man who came to work here. Your mum lived in Seagull Bay, so when the annual summer bar-b-q was held, and Nicola was the woman chosen to be auctioned off for an hour-long date for charity, your father bid alongside the local men. It was quite a to-do. You see, because your father lived outside the community, everyone put their penny's worth in saying it shouldn't be allowed—someone from outside the community entering the auction that is. Much like these days, the community sticks together. Nothing has changed in that respect. The downside is, they all still put their penny's worth in.'

Tammy was captivated by the story. She had always wondered about her parents' early years, and this was a piece of their history even her Uncle Ben didn't know. 'Wow.'

'Anyway, it was quite the event. Your father bid fiercely, and in the end, he won. Your mother had to spend an hour with him on a date at the barbecue. That was it. The love spell had been cast over both of them. After that, they were inseparable. Phil and I became very good friends with them. We used to double date. I've actually got some photos somewhere. I'll find them out and bring them to the barbecue.'

Pamela continued, 'Your mother's parents didn't quite approve of your father back then. They thought he was an outsider, you see. Your great uncle Ben used to stick up for your father, but they still wouldn't accept him. But your father, he was determined. He even proposed in front of the whole community the following year at the next barbecue.'

Tammy's eyes sparkled with interest. 'Proposed at the barbecue auction?'

Pamela nodded. 'Yes, it was quite the event. Your father not only won your mother's heart that day he won the hearts of the whole community. I guess that's why they all went to their wedding.'

Tammy couldn't help but smile at the romantic tale. 'That's a wonderful story.'

Pamela winked. 'Love has a way of finding its path, even when there are obstacles. It's a lesson I've seen play out in the lives of many who live here.'

As they chatted further about her parents and the farm, Tammy felt an even deeper connection to her roots and a sense of nostalgia. Pamela's stories filled in some of the gaps in her understanding of her family's history, and it was a gift she hadn't expected.

When it was time to leave the farm shop, Tammy said her goodbyes to Pamela and Ruby, promising to bring the cupcakes for the upcoming barbecue.

Outside, Mina was waiting in her car. Arms full of ingredients for her cakes, Tammy could just about see over the top of them. As she approached Mina's car, she noticed a familiar car pulling up not far from them. Her stomach clenched into a tight ball. It was her ex-boyfriend. Panic surged through her veins. She hadn't seen him since their breakup, and she certainly hadn't expected to encounter him now—not here.

Tammy quickly ducked down beside Mina's car, her heart pounding. The window on the passage side whirred down. 'Tammy, are you alright? What are you doing down there?'

'Mina, it's Richi,' she whispered urgently.

Mina glanced at her with concern. 'Richi? Who is Richi? Are you hiding down there from him?'

'Richi is my ex. How did he find me here?'

Mina gasped. 'You *are* hiding? Are you in some sort of victim protection programme?'

'No. Nothing like that.' Tammy whispered. 'Has he seen me?'

'I don't think so. He's going into the shop.'

Tammy quickly climbed into the car, putting her purchases into the footwell. She looked over at Richi's car. He was nowhere to be seen. 'Quick. Go into the shop Mina and see what he wants!'

'What?!'

'Please. Just pretend you need to buy something.' Tammy noticed her voice was trembling.

'Why don't *you* go back in?'

'Because I just don't want to see him right now, that's why.'

'Okay. I'll go. I'll be as quick as I can.'

'Thanks Mina.'

Mina climbed out and Tammy stayed low, keeping hidden. She listened out for the shop door opening, but all she could hear were the farm's cows mooing in a nearby field.

A few minutes later, Tammy heard the shop door open and close. She waited with bated breath and nearly jumped out of her skin when Mina opened the driver-side door and got in.

'He's talking to Pamela about a meeting he has with Pharis.'

'Pharis?' Tammy felt her blood boil. Why would Pharis be meeting up with her ex? 'Did he say what he wanted?'

'No, he just said he'd arranged to meet Pharis at the shop and—Oo, he's coming out.'

Tammy watched Mina as she followed Richi with her eyes. 'What's he doing now?'

'He's walking back to his car... Now he's getting in.' Tammy heard an engine firing into life. 'Now he's driving away. We'll wait a bit, Tammy. Make sure he's gone before we leave.'

Tammy sank lower in her seat, her mind racing with a mixture of emotions. She couldn't help but wonder why Richi had come looking for her. What did he want? He already had the apartment, the car, and the business. What more could he get from her?

As they waited in tense silence, Tammy couldn't shake the feeling that her past was colliding with her present in unexpected ways, and she had no idea where this collision would lead.

Chapter sixteen

The day of the summer barbecue at the farm had finally arrived, and Tammy found herself in the backseat of Mina's car with her uncle in the passenger seat. Beside her were two large trays filled with cupcakes she had lovingly baked and frosted for the occasion. The early afternoon sun cast a warm, golden hue over the rolling fields, and the gentle breeze carried the scent of freshly cut grass through the open car windows.

Uncle Ben glanced back at her from the passenger's seat, concern etched in the wrinkles of his weathered face. 'You've been quiet all morning, Tammy. Is everything all right?'

Tammy forced a smile, her thoughts filled with the events of the past week. She couldn't bring herself to tell Uncle Ben about the unexpected sighting with Richi at the farm shop, and she was yet to see Pharis and confront him about the meeting he'd had with her ex. Instead, she replied, 'I'm just a little nervous my cupcake icing is going to melt in this heat Uncle Ben, that's all.'

Mina scoffed, 'Those lovely little pieces of sugary heaven won't get a chance to melt Tammy. They'll be gone within ten minutes.'

Her uncle chuckled. 'Mina's right. You're going to do great with those cupcakes. Everyone's going to love them.'

Tammy chatted more animatedly for the rest of the ride, pushing thoughts of Richi from her mind. She wouldn't let him spoil this lovely event.

Ten minutes later, they arrived at the sprawling farm. The air was filled with the scent of mouth-watering grilled meats and the cheerful sounds of live folk music and laughter as they pulled to a stop.

Tammy got out and smoothed out invisible creases in her dress before reaching back into the car for the cupcakes. Mina stuck her head out of the window. 'I'll see you in a little while. I've got to go and fetch the hubby and the kids.'

Uncle Ben paid the fare. 'Bye Mina, see you shortly.'

'Yes, see you soon. Thanks, Mina,' Tammy gave her a bright smile.

With music blaring, the excited laughter of children, and lots of people mingling, Tammy could see the summer barbecue at the farm was in full swing. Walking alongside her uncle, they headed into the throng of it, towards a long table laden with finger foods.

Tammy looked left and saw Pharis heading their way. He was wearing a chequered shirt and jeans, and Tammy couldn't help but notice how the shirt strained tight across his exceptionally wide chest. 'Tammy, Ben, glad you could make it.' he said warmly, clasping Ben's hand in his and shaking it heartily. 'Great shin-dig, Pharis.' Said Ben.

Pharis looked directly into Tammy's eyes and she became quite taken aback by the intensity of his gaze. 'Can I help you get those cupcakes set up on the food table?'

'That would be so kind of you,' Tammy replied, hoping she seemed normal. She was desperate to give him the inquisition about his meeting with Richi when she found an opportune moment.

Pharis took the trays and found a space on the table nearby. Within seconds, children appeared from everywhere and milled around the table to claim a cupcake.

'Just take one each,' instructed Pharis, 'and don't forget to thank Tammy for your cupcakes.'

Tammy's heart melted when numerous sets of eyes looked up at her. The children nodded and thanked her, walking away with gleams in their eyes.

'Awww, you're welcome,' Tammy called after them.

Ben leaned over, trying to look through the crowd. 'I've just seen Ned. I'll be back in a bit.'

'Don't rush back on my account Uncle Ben, you go and mingle.'

Happy families, couples, and friends were gathered everywhere for the fundraiser.

Relaxing slightly, Tammy allowed herself to take in the festive surroundings. Long picnic tables were laden with potluck dishes and freshly picked produce. Children frolicked with farm animals in a petting area while adults mingled, sipping cold drinks. Across the field, Declan was manning a beverage stand. Catching Tammy's eye, he gave an enthusiastic thumbs up at the sight of her cupcakes being demolished by children. Tammy couldn't help smiling and waving back, his cheerful grin infectious as always.

Standing amid the vibrant festivities, she thought it was an opportune time to speak to Pharis. Cupcake in hand and a forced smile on her lips, her heart felt heavy, a mixture of tension and anticipation swirling within her. She turned to him opening her mouth to ask him about Richi, but then Declan appeared to her left. Pharis' smile faded. Tammy sighed, wishing the escalating rivalry between them didn't make every interaction so awkward.

Declan's eyes locked onto hers. 'Wow! You look absolutely stunning.'

Tammy's heart did a somersault. He was wearing a crisp white shirt rolled up at the cuffs and Tammy glimpsed strong forearms with tattoos peeking out just below.

'Thank you. You don't clean up too bad yourself.'

Pharis coughed. 'I'm not interrupting anything here, am I?' sarcasm dripped off every word.

Declan and Tammy shot each other looks just as Pamela, the gracious host approached, looking like an angel in a floaty cream dress.

'Tammy dear! So glad you're here,' she effused, clasping Tammy's hands warmly. 'I have some news for you. The ladies and I have picked you for the fundraiser this year. It's for a wonderful cause, the children's hospital.'

Tammy's brow furrowed, not quite sure what she meant. 'Excuse me?'

'You are the lucky lady. Some lucky fellows will be bidding to have an hour-long date with you this evening at the charity auction.'

Tammy blinked, her mind racing to catch up. 'Charity auction?'

Pamela nodded. 'Yes, do you remember me telling you about your parents and the auction? Well, you are the chosen woman from the community. You're our nominee this year.'

Tammy's eyes widened in surprise. 'Oh, I... I don't know if I can—'

Pamela cut her off gently. 'It's all in good fun, Tammy. And for a good cause. It will be commencing very shortly.'

Tammy's eyes widened in alarm, but Pamela was already gently propelling her towards the makeshift stage before she could object. This was not an ideal situation if Richi was lurking around somewhere.

'O-oh, I'm not sure...' Tammy stammered, but Pamela waved off her protests.

'Nonsense, the crowd will be thrilled! What sweetheart wouldn't want the chance to win a date with our town's newest darling?'

Before she knew it, Tammy found herself smiling awkwardly under the hot sun as the auctioneer called her name and recited a glowing—if rather exaggerated—description of her many charms and talents using flourishing language.

As expected, Declan and Pharis immediately leaped into fierce bidding, attempting to outspend each other. Under different circumstances, Tammy might have found their competitiveness over her flattering. But right now, she was just desperate for this circus to be over with.

The frantic bidding war waged on. Each bid was a testament to the chemistry she had felt with both of them, and her heart raced as the numbers climbed higher and higher.

Mixed emotions churned within Tammy. On one hand, she felt the undeniable pull of attraction toward both Pharis and Declan. On the other hand, her heart was still scarred from the wounds of her past with Richi, and the fear of being hurt again gnawed at her.

Each was standing on the opposite side of the field and heads were turning left to right, as if they were watching a tennis match as the bidding war raged. Declan and Pharis shot each other heated glares while the crowd watched, enthralled by their rivalry.

Just when Tammy thought the price couldn't possibly go any higher, a new voice called out casually, 'Five hundred pounds' from the back of the crowd. Tammy's stomach dropped into her feet—that cocky tone was unmistakable anywhere.

Sure enough, to her horror, Richi emerged from the throng flashing an insolent grin. Pamela clapped delightedly at the unexpected donation as Declan and Pharis exchanged stunned, worried glances. They both recognised that this mystery bidder spelled trouble.

Cheeks burning, Tammy had no choice but to go through with the 'date' as Richi swaggered to the front. He grabbed two beers from the drinks table Declan had been manning and strolled past him with an arrogant wink.

'I'll take it from here, buddy,' he muttered, loud enough for Declan to hear. Tammy saw Declan's jaw clench, but he held himself back with effort, shooting Tammy a sympathetic look.

Richi wasted no time steering Tammy toward an empty picnic table, where curious eyes followed their every move. Tammy saw her Uncle Ben storm over to Pharis and start talking to him. Her heart thundered in her chest and her palms felt clammy. 'You're looking as gorgeous as ever, Tam,' Richi said as he sat, leaning into her space.

Tammy recoiled from his cloying cologne. 'Let's not make small talk Richi,' she said tersely. 'What are you doing here?'

'I actually came here on business, then I spotted you in Seagull Bay.' He looked around at the crowd with a patronising glare. 'I never expected you to lower yourself this much, running off to this little backward seaside town.' Tammy bristled.

'Well, what I do is no longer your concern, so now you can leave,' Tammy said coldly. 'We have nothing more to discuss.'

At that, Richi's facade of charm instantly crumbled. 'You don't belong here. I see that now. You need to come back with me—I want you back. No, I need you back. The business is struggling without you.'

Tammy scoffed, astonished by his audacity. He'd thrown her away like garbage and now things weren't so good he thought he could reclaim her. 'No. I'll never set foot anywhere near you or that business again.'

Richi grabbed her wrist in a painful grip. 'I'm giving you one chance to forget this backwater place and come back where you belong.'

In her peripheral vision, Tammy saw Declan and Pharis both moving forward towards her, but Tammy quickly yanked her arm from Richi's grasp and stood up. 'The only place I belong is right here, as far from you as possible,' she retorted, voice shaking. 'Now get out of my sight, before a seventy-nine-year-old man puts you to shame.' Tammy looked over at her Uncle Ben who was poised ready to jump to her aid at any moment.

For a second, she thought Richi might get physical. Declan and Pharis appeared by her side simultaneously, their expressions fierce and protective. Declan's command was firm. 'Let her go!'

Pharis' large hand appeared and clamped firmly down on his shoulder. Richi didn't even get a chance to protest before Pharis swiftly escorted him away. Tammy blinked back angry tears as Ben rushed to her side.

'Are you alright? Who was that scoundrel?' he asked worriedly, scanning the dispersing crowd for the man's face.

'No one worth the trouble,' Tammy answered quickly. 'I'm fine, Uncle Ben, truly.' She hugged him, hoping to keep him from pursuing Richi.

After Ben reluctantly rejoined the party at Tammy's request, Declan appeared by her side, tentatively laying a hand on her back. 'That took real courage, standing up to him like that', he said quietly.

Tammy let out a shaky breath, allowing his gentle praise to soothe her frayed nerves.

They both looked up as Pharis approached, his usually carefree expression sombre. 'Declan, might I have a quick word with Tammy alone?' he asked.

Declan glanced between them before giving Tammy's hand a supportive squeeze. 'Of course. I'll be right over there if you need me,' he assured her kindly before stepping away.

Tammy steeled herself. She needed to know about Pharis' meeting with Richi. If he'd told him where she was. Her voice trembled with anger. 'How do you know Richi?'

'What? You know him too? I thought he was coming on strong to you just now.'

'Don't play innocent, Pharis,'

'I'm not. I've never seen him before in my life until Thursday. He scheduled a meeting with me to place a contract for produce from the shop.'

The penny dropped. 'Oh.' Tammy suddenly felt foolish.'

'How do you know him, Tammy?'

'He's my ex.'

'Ahhh. That makes sense then.' He glanced over at Declan, standing patiently to the side.

Tammy suddenly had a feeling Pharis intended to express his romantic intentions now that her ex and Declan were temporarily out of the picture. But his next words surprised her.

'You know Tammy, while I think you are insanely gorgeous, and I've come to care for you a great deal these past few weeks, I see now that it's Declan who truly holds your heart,' he said with a bittersweet smile. 'I've seen the way you both look at each other, and I know that you could never look at me the same way. Therefore, I'm going to stop pursuing something I know is never going to happen between us, and I wish you both every happiness together.'

'Wha—' He pulled her into a warm, almost brotherly embrace. Tammy was touched by his selfless gesture. 'Your friendship means the world to me Pharis,' she replied softly.

Pharis nodded, the smile returning to his eyes. 'And yours too. Look. I know it appears to you that Declan and I have this rivalry going on. He wasn't born in this community but he's a hundred percent part of it. I've not known Declan for long, but I can say with my hand on my heart that he's one of the good guys. He's caring, loyal, and I'm a bit miffed to say this, but hotter than me as well.' Tammy giggled. 'Now go on over to that man who wants to be yours more than anything, because I know you definitely want to be his.'

Tammy frowned with a smile as she looked up into Pharis' face. 'And how could you possibly know that?'

'Because you look at him the same way he looks at you, so go put him out of his misery,' he said, nodding towards where Declan waited pensively.

Tammy glanced at Declan. This time her heart and her head screamed, YES.

Chapter seventeen

Tammy turned to see Declan watching her from a distance, his expression tentative and worried. As she walked towards him, his stiff body language was like a beacon for his inner feelings. It was evident he hadn't liked her private talk with Pharis.

'Are you okay? What did Pharis want?'

'Oh, he's just looking out for a friend.'

Declan nodded and begrudgingly admitted something she'd never thought she'd hear him say. 'Yes, he does hold you in very high regard. You-you wouldn't go wrong in choosing a great guy like Pharis.' Tammy chuckled and Declan folded his arms defensively across his chest 'What's so funny?'

Tammy poked a finger delicately into his rock-hard abs. 'The friend he was looking out for is you, you idiot,' she giggled, 'and he said exactly the same... He told me what a great guy you are and that I should—'

Declan's brow shot up. 'Should what?'

'—I should put you out of your misery.'

Declan's eyes flitted all over Tammy's face. 'Out of my misery? And what suppose do you think he means by that?'

Tammy grabbed hold of his folded arms and pulled them free. His arms dropped unsure by his sides, and she intertwined her fingers in his.

Declan's mouth dropped open as he looked down at their linked hands. As his face slowly lifted, the change in his demeanour was instant. His eyes danced and the corners of his mouth tugged up like the sun rising over the horizon. He looked earnestly into Tammy's eyes. 'I know you've been hurt before, but I want to reassure you, I'll never take your trust for granted.' He lifted her hand and kissed the spot of her missing fingertip before delicately pushing back her hair to reveal the scar on her forehead. Leaning forward, he gently kissed that too.' Tammy fought to stop her eyes from welling up as he pulled away to look at her again. 'I want to protect you, Tammy. I want to make your world a better place. You are such a beautiful and wonderful person, and you deserve nothing but the best.'

Tammy choked back her tears. 'And so do you. I-I can't promise to give you my all straight away Declan, Richi really knocked the stuffing out of me, but what I can promise you is, over time, when the foundations of our relationship grow stronger, I'll be ready for more.'

His smile stretched from ear to ear. 'That's good enough for me, I'm a very patient man.' He looked past Tammy, to Pharis, who'd been joined by Ben. Tammy followed his eyes. Pharis and Ben stood side-by-side watching them with grins that would put the Cheshire cat from the movie *Alice in Wonderland* to shame.

Declan's tone was bright. 'I feel a little bit like the entertainment here. Should I get down on one knee and serenade you?'

Tammy burst out laughing and playfully nudged him. 'Don't you dare!'

Pamela walked over to them surrounded by a group of women. 'Are you alright Tammy? Pharis told me that the awful man was a new client of his. I can't believe he grabbed you like that.' The women reached out and touched her with soft, reassuring squeezes that held genuine care, their eyes brimming with empathy. Tammy felt very honoured to be on the receiving end of their compassion.

'I'm fine, really. It's a bit embarrassing, but he's actually my ex-boyfriend. I think seeing him here and him winning the bid to have a date with me was a coincidence.'

Pamela huffed and her back straightened indignantly. 'Well, he's no new client anymore. Pharis has just given him a piece of his mind. I dare say he and Ben would have given him much more if the ladies and I hadn't intervened.'

Tammy was shocked. She disliked Richi with a passion, but she wouldn't wish anything bad on him. She was glad nothing more had come of the incident; her uncle could have got really hurt and she would never have forgiven herself. She was just grateful they had her back.

As she was the cause of all the fuss, Tammy felt a need to get things back to normality. 'I'm sorry for all this fuss. Let's just enjoy the rest of the day, because it's most definitely the best summer barbecue I've ever been to.'

Right on cue, the folk band started playing again and locals, recognising the tune, screamed for joy and dragged each other onto the woodchip area designated for dancing. Tammy pulled herself out of her comfort zone and grabbed Declan's hand, dragging him to join the small throng of people now dancing to the merry tunes.

Pharis was soon at their side, dancing with a local girl and Ben walked on with a lady Tammy had seen buying fish from him. They took positions, his arm around her waist and her hand resting on his shoulder, their other hands clasped together as if they were about to do a waltz, then Tammy watched on amused as they jived slowly to the music.

Pharis leaned over. 'Wow! Your uncle's got moves I didn't think possible for a seventy-nine-year-old.'

Tammy giggled. 'I'm as shocked as you are. I just hope it's in the genes because I sure hope I'm as agile as him when I'm that age.'

As the lively folk music filled the warm summer air, Tammy, Declan, Pharis, and Ben found themselves twirling and swaying to the cheerful tunes. It was a heartwarming sight, a testament to the unity and camaraderie that Seagull Bay had to offer.

Tammy couldn't help but marvel at the scene around her. The farm's picturesque setting, the vibrant decorations, and the joyful laughter of the locals created an atmosphere of pure bliss. It was a stark contrast to the tumultuous events earlier in the day.

Pharis and his dance partner, Ben and his lady friend, and Tammy with Declan formed a little circle within the larger group of dancers. They moved in harmony with the music, their steps synchronised with the infectious energy of the moment.

As they danced, Tammy couldn't help but steal glances at Declan. His smile was infectious, and his eyes sparkled with joy. It was moments like these that made her grateful for the unexpected turn her life had taken.

The music played on into the night and the dancing continued. As the sun began to set, casting a golden glow over the farm, Tammy felt a deep sense of contentment. It was as if the troubles of the past had been washed away by the pure happiness of the present.

Declan, still holding Tammy's hand, spun her around in a playful twirl, and she couldn't help but laugh. His energy was infectious, and it was impossible not to get swept up in the moment.

As the dance came to an end, Tammy found herself back in Declan's arms, her heart pounding with a mixture of exhilaration and affection. They gazed at each other, the unspoken connection between them stronger than ever.

Pharis and Ben joined them, their smiles wide and their spirits high. It was a moment of pure joy, a reminder that sometimes life has a way of surprising you with unexpected beauty.

Pamela approached the group, her eyes filled with pride. 'I must say, you all make quite the charming dancers.'

Tammy blushed and gave a shy smile. 'It's all thanks to the wonderful music and atmosphere you've created here Pamela.'

Pamela beamed with delight. 'I'm so glad you're enjoying yourself, dear. That's what these gatherings are all about—bringing people together, creating memories, and celebrating life.' Tammy watched her with admiration as she made her way from guest to guest, thanking them for attending.

As the sun set and the sky turned shades of pink and orange, the atmosphere at the farm continued to be filled with joy and laughter. The aroma of grilled food mingled with the sound of lively conversation and the cheerful melodies from the folk band. The community had come together to celebrate, and Tammy couldn't help but feel grateful for the support and warmth she had found in Seagull Bay. It was a night to remember, a night that solidified the bonds between them all.

Dancing continued, and Tammy found herself letting go of her worries and immersing herself in the moment. With Declan's arms around her and Pharis by their side, she felt a sense of belonging that she hadn't experienced in a long time. The past was behind her, and the future held promise and hope.

The night wore on, the stars appeared in the sky, and the bonfire crackled with flames, casting a warm glow over the gathering. People shared stories, laughter, and delicious food. Tammy and Declan took a break from dancing to sit by the fire, their fingers intertwined, and they watched the flames dance.

'You know,' Declan said softly, 'I never imagined that moving here would lead me to all of this. Like you, circumstances brought me here, and it's the best thing that ever happened to me.'

Tammy turned to him, a soft smile playing on her lips. 'All of what?'

He gestured to the lively scene around them—the dancing, the laughter, the community coming together. 'This. A place where people truly care for each other. A place where I've found not just a job, but friends, and maybe even...' He trailed off, his gaze fixed on her.

'Maybe even what?' Tammy prodded gently, her heart pounding and the butterflies in her stomach coming to life.

Declan's expression was earnest as he met her gaze. 'Maybe even a chance at something that will last a lifetime. With you.'

Tammy's breath caught, her heart soaring with a mixture of emotions. 'Declan, I...'

Before she could finish her sentence, he leaned in and gently pressed his lips against hers. It was a soft, sweet kiss, filled with all the unspoken feelings they had been sharing throughout the day. It was a kiss that held promise, hope, and the possibility of something beautiful.

When they pulled away, Tammy looked into Declan's eyes, her heart in her throat. 'I'm scared, Declan. Scared of getting hurt again.'

Declan's fingers brushed against her cheek, his touch gentle and reassuring. 'Tammy, I understand. I've been hurt too. But sometimes, taking a chance on happiness is worth the risk.'

Tears welled up in Tammy's eyes, and she leaned into his touch, her heart overflowing with emotions. 'You're right. I don't want to let fear control my life.'

Declan smiled, his eyes filled with tenderness. 'We can take things one step at a time, at your pace. I'll be here for you, no matter what.'

As the night grew darker and the celebration continued, Tammy and Declan danced under the stars, their steps in sync with the beating of their hearts. The world around them faded away, leaving only the two of them in their own little bubble of happiness, and as the bonfire's glow illuminated their surroundings, Tammy couldn't help but feel that maybe, just maybe, this was the beginning of something truly special—a love story that bloomed in the most unexpected of places, surrounded by the warmth of a tight-knit community and the promise of a brighter future.

The growl of a big engine made them all turn, and Tammy's face lit up when she saw her uncle sitting on a hay bale in the back of a long trailer, alongside other locals, being pulled by a tractor with Phil, Pharis' father at the steering wheel. It had fairy lights wrapped all around the edge of the truck and it looked charming. Tammy sighed happily.

'All aboard. This is Phil's last run back to Seagull Bay,' called out Ben.

Declan grabbed Tammy's hands. 'Come on. It's a long way back to town, and as cute as you are, I could probably only manage piggybacking you half the way there. I think I've had one cider too many.'

Pharis came over and patted Declan affectionately on the back. 'You and me both buddy. Thankfully, it's Sunday tomorrow and you can have a lie-in.'

Declan shook his head. 'Not me. It's my rota for Sunday lunches.'

Tammy leaned into Pharis for a hug. 'Thanks for such a great day and thank your mum again for me.'

'I will.'

Declan and Pharis embraced, patting each other on the back. Phil sounded out a horn, startling everyone, and then laughed heartily at his own mischief.

Pharis laughed. 'Dad! You almost gave me a heart attack.'

'Just make sure that fire is out before I get back will you, son?'

Pharis held his thumb up in reply.

Tammy led Declan towards the back of the trailer. 'Come on. I don't know about you giving me a piggyback, I think it would be the other way around.'

The ride back to town was slow and magical—the perfect end to the day. Snuggled up against Declan, they listened to some of the locals as they sang a lullaby to their children. Tammy looked on contentedly before turning her eyes up to the stars.

'Yes. They're looking down on you now, Tammy. Chris and Nicola are happy because you are happy again.'

Her Uncle Ben's soft voice wrapped around her like a soft blanket. Tammy smiled warmly at her uncle. She hoped he knew that he was the catalyst for her newfound happiness.

Chapter eighteen

After saying their goodnights to Declan, Ben and Tammy began their final walk home. 'Shall we take a quick stroll on the beach Uncle Ben?'

Ben looked out at the sea with a grin. 'I never turn down the chance to be by the sea, lass. Aye. A walk along the beach would be grand.'

Together they headed for the beach, the gentle sea breeze caressing their skin. At that moment, Tammy felt certain of one thing; here in Seagull Bay was exactly where she was meant to be.

As they strolled, their feet sinking into the soft sand, Tammy couldn't help but reflect on her journey. 'You know, Uncle, I've realised that Seagull Bay has a way of weaving the past, present, and future together.'

Uncle Ben nodded, his eyes twinkling. 'Indeed, it does. It's a place that welcomes newcomers, cherishes memories, and fosters new beginnings. And you, my dear, have become an integral part of its story.'

Tammy leaned her head on his shoulder, feeling content. 'I'm grateful for everything—for you, for this town—for Declan, and for the chance to create something meaningful.'

Uncle Ben placed an arm around her, his touch reassuring. 'And remember, you're never alone. Your parents are always with you, watching over you.'

As the stars began to twinkle in the night sky, Tammy closed her eyes, feeling the presence of her parents in the gentle breeze. She knew that Seagull Bay had not only given her a tearoom but had also given her a second chance at love, family, and the beauty of life itself.

'Uncle Ben?'

'Yes, Tammy?'

'I want you to know. Although we've only really got to know each other these past few weeks...I can't thank you enough for all your generosity. It's weird but, I feel as though I've known you my whole life...I-I really care for you.'

'Oh, Tammy. You don't know how much you've made an old man happy. I love you as if you were my own daughter.' Tears magically appeared from nowhere and trickled down her cheeks. 'I've thanked God every day since your arrival for bringing you into my life. Now I'm praying He keeps me fit and healthy so I can enjoy some quality time with you and maybe even get to see our small gene pool extended.'

Tammy's giggle pushed past the lump in her throat. 'Hey, steady on. I've only just had my first kiss.' Ben chuckled.

'How come you never married Uncle Ben?'

He stopped walking and turned, looking out into the ocean. 'I found love once when I was young. But I was a fool and let her get away. Since then, the ocean has been the love of my life. But better to live and love and take the chance, than to let the chance of love slip away. A day of love is better than a lifetime without it. You take my word for it. I let my love get away and I've regretted it ever since.' He turned to look at Tammy. 'Life is short, Tammy. You never know what curveball it will throw your way. So, take some advice from this old sea dog. Enjoy every day as if it were your last. Live and love.' He smiled warmly and tapped the end of her nose. 'Now, come on. A warm mug of cocoa is calling my name from a cosy little cottage up on the hill.'

Tammy chuckled and linked arms with her uncle as he led her off the beach. Her heart was full of love and gratitude. She was going to take her uncle's advice. She looked back over her shoulder and whispered into the night, 'Thank you, Seagull Bay. Thank you for everything.'

As the stars began to twinkle in the darkening sky, Tammy felt a sense of gratitude wash over her. She had come to Seagull Bay seeking a fresh start, and what she had found was so much more—a community that welcomed her with open arms, true friends who had her back, and a tantalising connection with Declan that had the potential to blossom into something beautiful.

Tammy had a home and a new business; she was no longer alone—she had a family now...and she'd found love. She was excited to see what her future was going to be like in Seagull Bay. Katherine was right. Seagull Bay knew exactly what was right for its residents.

THE NEXT MORNING, WHILE her Uncle Ben was out visiting a neighbour, Tammy sat at the kitchen table sipping her tea whilst basking in the warm glow of the morning sun as it filtered in through the window. A smile pulled up the corners of her mouth as she quietly contemplated the tender kiss she'd shared with Declan.

Music outside caught her attention and curiosity pulled her to the front door. Opening it, she was shocked to see Declan leaning against his motorbike, whilst sweetly serenading her on an acoustic guitar. His fingers danced on the strings, producing a melody that filled the air with a sense of longing and love. Tammy's tummy fluttered and she couldn't help but smile at the sight of him. He looked smoking hot in his leather jacket and blue jeans, the emotion in his eyes matching every word of his serenade, his voice rich and velvety and as soothing as the morning breeze.

Tammy stepped outside, her heart swelling with affection as Declan sang about reuniting with a long-lost love. His lyrics were filled with emotion, and she could feel every word deep within her soul. She didn't recognise herself as the same person who'd travelled her on the train not long ago—the woman who was so anti-men As Declan finished the song, he looked at her with a twinkle in his eye.

'That was beautiful, Declan,' Tammy said, her voice filled with admiration.

He grinned, his guitar resting against his chest. 'I'm glad you liked it, Tammy. It just felt...right this morning.' He took a few steps forward and placed his guitar behind the fence and retrieved two helmets. Offering one to Tammy with a lopsided smile, he suggested, 'How about a little adventure today? A motorbike ride through the countryside?'

Tammy's eyes lit up with excitement. 'I'd love that! I've never been on a motorbike before.'

They hopped on Declan's motorcycle and Declan fired the engine to life. As they began their journey, Tammy was impressed at how skilfully Declan manoeuvred the bike around town before taking it onto the main road. Soon they were winding along leafy country lanes.

Tammy was pleasantly surprised when she heard Declan's voice in her ear. The helmets had radio intercom installed and Declan pointed out and shared stories about each of the children's homes and foster placements he had called home since going into care. His voice held a mix of nostalgia and reflection, and Tammy listened with rapt attention, knowing this was important to him.

'This is where I stayed with an old friend before moving into Katherine's flat above the shop,' he said, gesturing to a quaint cottage by the river. 'We had some great times here, fishing and taking Fernando for long walks as we chewed the fat together.'

Tammy smiled, imagining Declan and his friend creating cherished memories in that peaceful setting with a big fluffy Fernando in the mix of things.

Further down the road, they passed a cosy farmhouse nestled among rolling hills. Declan's voice softened as he spoke. 'I spent a year here, helping out with the farm. It was hard work, but it felt good to be part of something—a family again.'

Tammy could sense the significance of each place he mentioned, the bittersweet memories that had shaped his journey. She placed a comforting hand on his back as he shared his past.

Finally, they arrived at a small cottage at the end of a gravel road. He explained it was the last place he had lived before going into care. A man standing outside the front door waved a greeting to them before disappearing into a greenhouse in the side garden. Declan waved back as he came to a stop and took off his helmet. Tammy followed suit. He gestured for Tammy to get off the bike, and when she was safely on the ground, he got off and pulled the side-stand down.

'I've arranged for us to have a look around.'

Tammy pointed to the cottage. 'In there?'

Declan nodded and guided Tammy inside. She marvelled at the simple beauty of the space.

'This place holds so many memories.' Declan said, a hint of nostalgia in his voice. 'My sanctuary, my refuge. I cooked meals, read books, and daydreamed about the future right here.'

Tammy followed him as he pointed out various corners of the room, each with its own story. She could feel the weight of his memories, both joyful and painful.

Declan paused, his gaze lingering on the room that held so many fond moments. His eyes brimmed with emotion as he spoke of his parents and their unfulfilled promises, and of the day he went into care.

'When my parents went away, they promised they'd come back,' he said softly. 'But they never did. It felt like the darkness had taken them away forever.'

Tammy reached out, gently touching his arm. 'Declan. Was this your home?'

He turned to her, his eyes filled with vulnerability. 'Yes. It was here my life changed for the worst... But now, with you by my side, it feels like there's hope again.'

Tears welled up in Tammy's eyes as she hugged him tightly. In that small, humble cottage, surrounded by the echoes of his past, she realised that she was becoming a part of Declan's journey—a journey of healing, hope, and the possibility of a brighter future together and he was becoming a part of hers.

As Tammy held Declan close, their embrace was filled with a profound sense of understanding and connection. They had both carried their own burdens, their own scars from the past, and yet here they were, in this humble cottage, sharing a moment of vulnerability and hope.

Declan's voice was barely above a whisper as he continued, 'For the longest time, I felt like I was wandering in the dark, searching for something I couldn't quite grasp. But now, with you, it's as if I've found my way back into the light.'

Tammy pulled back slightly to look into his eyes, her own glistening with unshed tears. 'Declan, I've been through my share of hardships too. And meeting you, being with you, it's like discovering a missing piece of my own puzzle.'

Tammy's heart beat in harmony. It was as if their souls entwined in a moment that transcended words. Declan leaned in, his lips meeting hers in a tender, heartfelt kiss. It was a kiss filled with promises of a shared future, of healing, and of the love they were slowly building together.

When they finally pulled away, Declan whispered, 'Tammy, I want you to know that I'll always be here for you, through every high and low.'

Tears of gratitude and joy streamed down Tammy's cheeks as she replied, 'And I'll be here for you, Declan. We'll face whatever comes our way together.'

They held each other close once more, finding solace in the warmth of their embrace. In that small cottage, with the memories of the past and the promise of the future, they had discovered something precious—a love that had the power to heal and make their worlds brighter.

As they left the cottage hand in hand, ready to face the world together, Tammy couldn't help but feel that sometimes, life had a way of bringing two souls together, mending what was broken, and giving them a chance at a beautiful new beginning. With determination in her heart, she vowed to stand by Declan's side and help him in his quest to find his parents, no matter what challenges lay ahead. Together, they would create their own harmonious future, built on love, trust, and unwavering support. They had found their own sweet serenade—a love that would last a lifetime.

What's happening next in Seagull Bay?

Christine owns the local hair salon. Tom the plumber, has just ended an online relationship. He's hoping his relationship with Christine can be more than just good friends. Marcus has just started a new pet-grooming business inside Christine's shop.

What could go wrong?

Pre-order Finding Love in Seagull Bay now on Amazon!

Apple crumble with summer fruit and vanilla custard.

675 g Killinchy cooking apples (peeled, cored, and cut into chunks)

3 tablespoons of caster sugar

1 teaspoon of vanilla essence

115g plain flour

40g demerara sugar (plus 1 tablespoon for sprinkling)

45g cold butter (diced)

4 tablespoons of porridge or muesli

150g of blackberry

150g of raspberry

150g of figs

Preheat the oven to 200 degrees. Place the apples in a saucepan along with the caster sugar, vanilla essence, and 2 tablespoons of water. Cook until soft. Don't be afraid to taste them halfway through as some people like them sweeter, if so, add a little more sugar. Transfer to a greased oven-proof dish.

For the crumble:

Place the flour, demerara sugar, and butter in a mixing bowl. Mix with your fingers or in a mixing bowl until the mix resembles a breadcrumb consistency.

Stir in the porridge or muesli, mix well, and scatter over the apples and the extra sugar. Bake for 45 minutes until golden brown.

For the custard:

100ml of double cream

350ml of whole milk

2 large egg yolks

1 1\2 teaspoons of cornflour

50g caster sugar

1 teaspoon of vanilla essence

Place the cream and milk in a saucepan and gently bring to slightly below boiling point. Gather a large mixing bowl and whisk the yolks, cornflour, sugar, and vanilla until the sugar has dissolved gradually. Pour into the hot milk and cream, whisking continuously. Wipe your saucepan and pour your mix back into it (chef's tip: slowly stir with a wooden spoon) until thickened.

Once the crumble is ready, if you want to make it look fancy gather a large round cutter and cut into the crumble. Place in the centre of the plate, spoon the custard around the plate, then arrange the fruit and dust with a little icing sugar. Serve and enjoy.

The author and Paul Watters accept no responsibility for what you feed yourself.

Follow Paul Watters for more tasty recipes on Instagram or Facebook.